What Goes Around...

Best Wishes
Paula Aird

By: PAULA AIRD
3 Apr 2005

© Copyright 2004 Paula Aird. All rights reserved.

No part of this publication may be reproduced, stored in a retrieval system, or transmitted, in any form or by any means, electronic, mechanical, photocopying, recording, or otherwise, without the written prior permission of the author. You may contact the author in care of publisher.

Printed in Victoria, Canada

This is a work of fiction. It is set partially in the Caribbean island of Grenada, but in some instances locations are given fictitious names. All characters, with the exception of well known public figures, are a product of the author's imagination and any resemblance to persons, living or dead, is purely coincidental.

Cataloguing Data:
Aird, Paula
What Goes Around...
Caribbean fiction
Grenada - fiction
Authors Canadian (English)

Note for Librarians A cataloguing record for this book that includes the U.S. Library of Congress Classification number, the Library of Congress Call number and the Dewey Decimal cataloguing code is available from the National Library of Canada. The complete cataloguing record can be obtained from the National Library's online database at: www.nlc-bnc.ca/amicus/index-e.html
ISBN 1-4120-1529-4

TRAFFORD

This book was published *on-demand* **in cooperation with Trafford Publishing.**
On-demand publishing is a unique process and service of making a book available for retail sale to the public taking advantage of on-demand manufacturing and Internet marketing. **On-demand publishing** includes promotions, retail sales, manufacturing, order fulfilment, accounting and collecting royalties on behalf of the author.

Suite 6E, 2333 Government St., Victoria, B.C. V8T 4P4, CANADA
Phone   250-383-6864   Toll-free   1-888-232-4444 (Canada & US)
Fax   250-383-6804   E-mail   sales@trafford.com
Web site   www.trafford.com
TRAFFORD PUBLISHING IS A DIVISION OF TRAFFORD HOLDINGS LTD.
Trafford Catalogue #03-1907   www.trafford.com/robots/03-1907.html

10   9   8   7   6   5   4

DEDICATION

This book is dedicated to the memory of my beloved parents, Cyril and Ermyntrude Benjamin, who nurtured, taught and loved me.

I have occasionally found myself the beneficiary of a kind word or deed because of some act of benevolence by my father or mother in the past. It has made me appreciate more fully the significance of the saying, "what goes around, comes around."

ACKNOWLEDGEMENTS

Daphne Charles - the first person to read and edit this manuscript. Donning the hat of an English teacher, she dug up old text books, rolled up her sleeves and went to work. Thanks for being so generous with your time, Daph. Your corrections and suggestions were invaluable. Above all I am most grateful to you for believing in this book and your constant and I mean *constant* words of support and encouragement.

Dawn Brown - those three words - *I loved it* - over the phone after you'd read the manuscript were a breath of fresh air. Thanks for being so positive about the book and for encouragement and advice. You were an inspiration.

Sincere thanks to H. Nigel Thomas for responding to the request of a stranger and reading the manuscript, despite a very busy schedule. I am grateful for all your positive comments which gave me a lift and for suggestions especially in the publishing arena.

Thanks to my family, especially Joan, Tanya and Marjorie, for your encouragement and believing I can do it. Kandia and Kevin - thanks for being my cheerleaders from the side lines and for your generous help with the technical aspects of this book. Keith - I am so grateful for your support, insightful suggestions and critiques which meant the world to me. Love and thanks to you all.

Above all I thank God from whom all blessings flow. If this project is meant to be, it simply will.

What Goes Around…

CHAPTER 1

"Jessica, is time you put down those books now and come out here to help us," Albertine snarled at her stepdaughter, who was studying in the back room of *Best Bargains* store, which Albertine owned with Jessica's father, Ian Farrow.

Jessica attended the St. George's Convent high school, and she was preparing to write the Cambridge O Level exams, the following week. Along with other participating students, she had been given the week off from classes to prepare for the upcoming exams. She was smack in the middle of revising the circulatory system, when Albertine interrupted.

"It busy?" Jessica asked, peering through the doorway of the back room. Observing that there was only one customer in the store, she continued "Daddy say I could study back here unless it get too busy in front."

"I don't care what yoh father say." Albertine's eyes flashed angrily at Jessica. "He gone gallivantin' and expect me and Flo to handle de store by weself."

In the sewing corner to the far right of the store, Fleurina Bailey noisily compressed the foot pedal of the sewing machine. She could feel Jessica looking in her direction but avoided eye contact, not wanting to be in the middle of a conflict between stepmother and daughter. Besides, she had these ten skirts to finish up by tomorrow morning, and that's what she was going to direct her attention to.

Jessica loudly slammed her biology book shut and almost toppled over a stool, as she emerged from the back room into the tiny grocery section of the store. A waist high counter separated her and the goods for sale from the customers.

"Yes Ma'am…what you want today?" she directed a phony smile in the lone customer's direction, just as Albertine disappeared into the back room, banging the door shut behind her.

"Ah half pound o' saltfish please, Miss." Jessica reached into the refrigerator and produced the salted cod fish, which was already packaged into half pound and one pound quantities. Amidst a lot of steupsing and criticism from Albertine, she had convinced her Dad that it was a good idea when it wasn't busy to parcel off some of the groceries into different quantities. It would save time at the point of serving the customer. What an excellent idea this was proving to be.

"Anything else?"

"Dat's all," answered the customer, as she pulled a dirty looking handkerchief from her brassiere. She untied it and slowly counted out the pennies and coins, which she gave to Jessica who deposited it in the cash machine. A few more people sauntered into the store. Some bought rice, flour and sugar, already parceled off.

"Sorry…we don't carry chicken and eggs anymore," Jessica apologized to one young man.

Some people didn't want to buy anything - they just wanted to chit chat. One poor woman wanted Jessica 'to trust' her some milk for her baby.

What on earth was taking Albertine so long in the back room, Jessica wondered. She was anxious to get back to her studies. *Come hell or high water I'm not going to flunk these O Level exams.* She certainly couldn't afford to, as it would mean having to live with her father and stepmother for yet another year. After five years of this, enough was enough. *The woman gets on my nerves practically every living day.*

"What's with the queen this mornin'?" she whispered to Flo, referring to Albertine.

"I think she goin' down to the hotels," Fleurina whispered back.

Just then Albertine sashayed out of the back room, decked off in a bright blue and yellow floral dress, with a wide brimmed yellow straw hat and matching handbag. Jessica noticed that she had applied fresh makeup, but declined from pointing out the little glob of lipstick stuck to her teeth.

"Until yoh father come back…you stay out here," she hissed at Jessica, who kept her head turned aloft, refusing to acknowledge the curt order.

"A lot of new tourists at the hotels," Albertine said to Fleurina, using a much softer tone. "I'm sure I'll be bringing back lots of orders" and hastily she left the store. In the next second they heard the door of her *Valiant* slam shut as the car sped down the steep hill.

Ian Farrow had started *Best Bargains* grocery store many years ago. At one time it was one of the more thriving businesses in the town. He sold fresh and salted meats, poultry, dairy products, dried goods as well as fresh fruit and vegetables. However, over the past few years, with competition springing up nearby, business in the grocery section of the store began diminishing. That section was being eroded more and more by the sewing section, which Albertine later started. Now, the grocery section carried only dried and canned goods and occasionally salted fish or meats.

    Albertine first began selling cloth, ribbons, threads and other sewing paraphernalia. but when she happened upon Fleurina whose expertise at the sewing machine was legendary, a new idea came to her. Together they formulated a few simple patterns, using bright, catchy fabric and began sewing custom made outfits. She targeted the tourists at the various hotels and was flabbergasted by the terrific response, especially as the outfits were guaranteed to be ready in forty eight and occasionally twenty four hours. There were wrap around skirts of various lengths, with or without matching tops, with or without sleeves, that opened at the back or front. Albertine discovered that the secret to success was developing simple patterns, having excellent workmanship and short, reliable turn around times.

    There were occasions when not only Jessica and Albertine had to join in to help with the sewing, but also Fleurina's mother and Madge, her younger sister, who was also Jessica's best friend. They would stay up all night putting the finishing touches on outfits. If 'push came to shove' Fleurina would even request help from Jessica's grandmother, Hilda Thorne, who besides being an excellent seamstress herself, lived up the hill from the Baileys. The problem was Fleurina was sure to hear the warning, "Make sure I get mih good share of de pay…okay? Dis not for free Darlin'…de creature done workin' Jessica to de bone already." Hilda Thorne reserved the term 'the creature' for anyone she disliked, which in this case was Albertine Farrow. The bottom line for Fleurina was competent, timely completion of the work.

"She got some nerve," Jessica commented angrily to Flo about Albertine.

"Maybe yoh father comin' back soon," Flo replied. Since she worked on commission, she wanted to finish the outfits that were currently in process, before Albertine returned with new orders. She certainly didn't want to have to leave her sewing to serve customers.

"Yesterday, I couldn't study because I had to mind children and clean house…today I have to work here…and she know I have big exams to prepare for," Jessica complained. She leaned on the counter, holding her head in her hands. Then looking at Fleurina, she asked "You t'ink dat right?"

Fleurina compressed the sewing machine pedal again. She made good money working for Albertine, whom she thought treated her very fairly. She didn't want to say anything that Jessica might quote to Albertine afterwards.

"Y'all watch me tomorrow," Jessica said threateningly to Flo's bent head, and underneath her breath, added "this damn nonsense about to stop."

****

At about two a.m. Jessica switched off the electric light in the room she shared with Debbie, her eight year old half-sister, and rolled into bed. Yes, she thought to herself contentedly, I have most of the biology down pat now. She pulled the covers over her head, hoping to induce sleep quickly, but the exams were still mulling around in her brain. I'll spend tomorrow studying *MacBeth*, she decided, and the next day I can devote entirely to geometry and algebra. To do this, Jessica was determined to spend the rest of her days off, studying at the convent. *The queen certainly wouldn't like it, but tough - that's how it's going to be.* She recalled the big fight between Albertine and her Dad, earlier that night.

    Obviously in a bad mood, Albertine thumped a few times on the door of the girls' bedroom, where Debbie was fast asleep, telling Jessica to turn off the light. It's already ten o'clock, she pointed out, and it's bad for little children's eyesight, to sleep with the light on. Nice one, thought Jessica, knowing full well that the electricity bill was probably what was irritating Albertine. Ian intervened and told her that was pure bullshit. Albertine exploded like a thunderbolt. She mentioned the fact that Ian had not spent more than five minutes in the store that entire day. She was tired of his shifty behavior. People were starting to look at her funny. Not to mention his goddam, t'ink-she-smart daughter, sitting on her arse in front some book all the time.

    In the girls' bedroom, Ian was lifting Debbie to put her to sleep in the adjoining room beside her little brother, Trevor. He seemed determined to ignore his wife's tirade, until the reference to Jessica. Then it was his turn to explode.

    "Jessica more than earn her keep in this house," he shouted. "Since she come here, how much you pay for maid…eh? She clean, she cook, she baby sit, she help in the store, she sew. What more you want…eh?"
Albertine was finally silent but Ian was now warmed up.

    "When was the last time you cook a meal in this house…eh?"

Still silence from Albertine.

"When was the last time you bathe Trevor...eh?" Ian was on a roll.

"Jessica bathe the children every night and help them with their homework too. All you do is complain, complain, complain." His voice was getting louder by the second. Jessica thought she could hear soft whimpering from Albertine. "So quit yoh damn complainin', woman. Ah sick of it!"

While Jessica was glad to have her father in her corner, she was embarrassed by his loud ranting and raving. She could see Mrs. DeCoutreau, the neighbour on their right, tilting her head, trying to hear exactly what was going on. She hoped Jack, Mrs. DeCoutreau's son and her 'heart throb', was not witnessing this tirade. All of a sudden, the neighbour across the road from them had turned off the radio and all was silent there, in an obvious effort to eavesdrop. She knew they would be the subject of much neighbourhood gossip - the butt of many jokes - for the next few days.

Jessica believed that her father was probably listening to cricket on the radio all day long with his buddies at *The Garage* - a hangout in Richmond that he frequented. Where cricket was concerned, Ian could lose himself for hours on end. The West Indies team was playing against England these days, and almost everyone on the island, was following the action. He was not engaged in 'shifty behavior' as Albertine had suggested. Yes, Jessica said to herself wearily, as she snuggled into her pillow, I can't wait to go back to the country to live in peace with Grandma again.

CHAPTER 2

Before Jessica started attending the convent she lived with her grandmother, Hilda Thorne, in Rockville. She had little to no recollection of her mother, Audrey, who died when Jessica was just three years old. Grandma had been the one, in whose arms she cuddled; around whose neck she clung, when a nurse wanted to give her a typhoid injection. As far as she was concerned, Grandma was her mother. But sometimes just before she was fully awakened from sleep, in that brief period of in between, a shadowed memory would surface, and she would see a thin, dark-skinned woman smiling at her. The woman would often be lying in bed and would smile weakly when she noticed Jessica. Jessica would wrestle with these thoughts afterwards. Was this a dream, she wondered, or a memory?

Neither did Jessica lack for siblings. She considered the Baileys, who lived down the hill from Grandma, to be her own brothers and sisters. Altogether there were ten Bailey siblings; some of the older ones had gone abroad or married and left home. Every once in a while a son or daughter would descend upon the household for a visit, with a spouse and a brood of young ones. It was amazing how the little bungalow just seemed to expand at those times. Jessica and Madge, the last of the Bailey girls, were born in the same year and had much in common. They were in the same class in elementary school. They were each other's confidantes. Jacob, one of the boys, was born mentally challenged but as far as the family was concerned, he was smart in many ways.

On the flat part of the hill, just by the side of Grandma's house, was the unofficial space where the neighbourhood children gathered to play cricket or rounders. The prolific goespoe tree at the back of the house not only provided juice for Grandma's lunch table but its hard young fruit acted as suitable balls for these games. The children learned to bat the ball accurately as it was 'an out' to hit any ball directly into the adjoining cocoa patch. Jacob usually preferred to field underneath the cocoa trees for these stray balls.

Five years ago, when the elementary school headmaster, passed by Grandma's with the terrific news, that Jessica had succeeded in the scholarship examination to go to high school, Jessica jumped with joy. A moment later, she was saddened when she learned that Madge, who also wrote the exams, had not been successful. There were about five hundred children all over the island competing for a scant fifty spaces.

"It's okay," said Madge, trying to hide her disappointment. She had come up the hill to congratulate Jessica. "I have another chance...I can write it again next year."

The day after the headmaster's news, the names of all the successful candidates appeared in the Grenada paper - *The West Indian*. Jessica couldn't help that feeling of pride when everywhere she went in the community, people were congratulating her and telling her how happy they were for her.

She would no longer be attending *Our Lady of Fatima Catholic Elementary school* that she had grown so accustomed to. The upper level of the school was one huge open hall with a picture of Queen Elizabeth II and the Pope at one end. At the other end was a stage which was the headmaster's domain. In between, the teachers positioned the black boards and the benches to create separate class rooms. The school day began with the entire student body assembled in the middle of the hall to say prayers and sing hymns like *Come Holy Ghost Creator Come*. Jessica was certainly going to miss this routine. She was going to miss all the different fruits country children brought to school with them - damsel, tamarind, pennypiss and sapodilla were some of her favorites. But she was looking forward to the new experience of going to school in town, where you could see the ships in the St. George's harbour. If only Madge could be with her.

****

Grandma got up early the following Saturday morning, and dressed herself in her best Sunday dress and hat. She wore her old garden shoes down the hill to the main road, not wanting to get mud on her good, red court shoes, which she slipped into before the bus arrived. She gave her garden shoes to Jessica to carry back home. Jessica didn't know it at the time but Grandma was about to pay a visit to Ian and Albertine's store in the town, armed with a copy of *The West Indian*.

"My...we lookin' spiffy dis mornin'," Lenox Bailey, the driver of the bus *Sensational*, commented on Grandma's appearance, teasingly.

Grandma pretended to scold Lenox. He was one of the Bailey children and she had known him since he was a baby.

"Boy, stop bein' so fresh and jus' drive de bus...okay?"

"Mus' be meetin' up wid de boyfriend today," Lenox continued to poke fun at Grandma, while the other passengers on the bus shook with laughter. Many of them carried large baskets with goods that they were going to sell in the market square. Grandma steupsed loudly.

"Look Boy...who you talkin' to like dat...eh? Careful ah don' put you cross me lap and whip yoh backside."

This light hearted sparring entertained the passengers for the entire journey. When Grandma eventually alighted from the bus, some passengers were emboldened sufficiently to say,

"Give boyfriend a nice hug an' kiss for we," and "Don' leh boyfriend tire you out too much."

On her arrival at *Best Bargains* store, Grandma greeted Ian and Albertine loudly.

"Good mornin' Mr. Farrow...Good mornin' ma'am...Hi Flo," she waved at Fleurina, who had started working for Albertine earlier that month. Ian nodded and returned the greeting. Fleurina smiled.

"Hello Ms Thorne...what can I get for you?" Albertine asked stiffly.

"It make so hot today," Grandma fanned herself with the newspaper.

"Is dat you Mama Thorne?" asked a customer standing by. "I see yoh little grand pass de scholarship exams. Dat so good!"

Grandma smiled broadly and accepted the congratulations, looking at Ian from the corner of her eye.

"Yes…Jessica done real good," Ian finally said, then added "I ain't see the papers yet…but…"

"Look de list o' names here." Grandma thrust the newspapers she was fanning herself with, to Ian. "Look her name right here…Jessica Farrow." She placed her finger exactly where Jessica's name was.

"Yes…yes…she done real good…see Albertine," he pointed the papers in the direction of his wife, who used that opportunity to bustle over another customer.

"I have another list," Grandma continued, taking a seat on a shabby but sturdy stool in front of the counter. "First, I start makin' arrangements for she to go to de convent."

Ian nodded.

"Next, I t'ink it best for she live wid her father in town, if she goin' to de convent."

Albertine gulped visibly. Grandma ignored her. "And she goin' to need school uniforms and books too."

"Live wid us?" Albertine finally composed herself enough to speak, then added, "But Flo takin' de bus every day an' it not killin' her."

"Why have her takin' de bus back and forth every day, when she can live wid her father in Willow Lane?" Grandma asked no one in particular. Willow Lane happened to be one of the more prestigious of the residential areas in the town.

"Yeh...I think that will be all right," said Ian, ignoring looks of protests from Albertine. The three-bedroom house in Willow Lane, left to him by his parents, would certainly have room enough for Jessica. "She can help with Debbie and some of the housework too," he added to placate his wife.

"Of course she gwine help...but remember, she not de maid," Grandma thought it prudent to get that fact in. Then after a brief pause she added, "If you give me de cloth for de uniforms I can sew dem meself." Thanks to Albertine's successful lobbying, *Best Bargains* was one of the designated suppliers of the uniform material in the town. The look of relief on Albertine's face did not escape Grandma. I guess she thought I was going to ask them to sew the uniforms too, she thought to herself with some amusement. Grandma continued.

"She have to buy a belt and tie at de convent." Ian nodded again. This was the first time in the thirteen years since Jessica was born that he was contributing anything towards her upkeep. In the deep recesses of his soul, he always harboured some guilty feelings about that. He had given Audrey a small amount of cash before the baby was born. He knew he would never marry her - a poor, dark-skinned, country girl - when there was the young, flashy Albertine, with pony tail bouncing off her back. After the baby was born, Audrey had simply disappeared - then he'd heard regretfully of her death.

"And she gwine need white socks and white shoes...one pair for rainy days and one pair for sunny days."

"My...how come we so fussy? Two pairs?" asked Albertine, screwing up her nose.

"That'll be fine," Ian interjected. "Get Flo to measure out the material," he instructed his wife.

Going over to Fleurina, in the sewing section, Albertine asked her to measure out material enough for four blouses and one skirt.

"Excuse me," interrupted Grandma loudly from the other side of the store. "She gwine need six blouses an' two skirts." Under her breath she added "Jessica not gwine be going to de convent lookin' like ragamuffin."

Albertine shot a dismayed look at Ian, who simply nodded his consent. Then going to the cash register, he withdrew some money which he gave to Grandma. "I hope this will cover the shoes an' other stuff, Ma Thorne. Come back if you need any more." Grandma thanked him, tied the money up in her handkerchief, which she then placed securely in her ample bosom. A few minutes later Fleurina handed her a bag containing the uniform material. With a loud 'God Bless' and 'Goodbye to all', Grandma left the store.

****

"You going to live in town!" Madge said excitedly to Jessica. She loved being the harbinger of breaking news.

"Whaat?" stammered Jessica in amazement. She was overwhelmed when Grandma returned from town that afternoon, with yards of white material for her school blouses and navy blue material for her pleated skirts. She had warned Jessica not to touch the material with dirty hands, but had mentioned nothing about her going to live in town.

"Yes…you going to live wid yoh father in Willow Lane."

Fleurina had told her sister Madge, who told Jessica all about Grandma's visit to the store that morning.

Over the next few weeks Jessica was happy, sad, excited, nervous and sometimes a combination of all four emotions at the same time. She was happy to be going to the convent. She couldn't wait to learn Spanish and biology and all those difficult subjects she'd heard about. She felt up to the challenge. Her knees weakened at the thought of going into new surroundings alone, without her best friend for comfort and reassurance. The buying of new shoes, socks, and underwear, the sewing of uniforms, all the hustle and bustle thrilled her. She was excited about going to live in town, especially in one of the grand houses of Willow Lane, where they had flush toilets and electricity but sad - very sad at leaving poor Grandma to live all by herself.

It was Madge again who broke the news to Jessica that Grandma wasn't going to be living alone. Grandma's younger sister and her son were coming from Gauvine to live with her. Jessica liked Aunt Mattie well enough - she always had some treat like guava cheese or peanut sweetie to offer Jessica, but the son, Abraham, who was two years older than Jessica, was a stout, sullen youth, who enjoyed picking his nose. She usually kept her distance from him.

"Whaat?" Jessica almost choked. "Who tell you this?"

"I hear Ma Hilly whisperin' it to Mammie."

"You sure you hear right?" Jessica felt herself becoming angry. Here she was feeling sorry for Grandma, who was in fact kicking her out to give her space to others.

"Yes," replied Madge. "It have somet'ing to do wid Aunt Mattie not hearin' from her husband for six years now."

"So?" Jessica couldn't make the connection. She'd heard Grandma talk many a time about Aunt Mattie's husband, whom she called a 'scamp' or 'dat wort'less Dawson.' She'd said that "de minute de scamp reach in England, after Mattie done sell dey land to make de passage money, he pick up wid some white woman and drop his wife and son like two bad penny." Still Jessica didn't understand what that had to do with them coming to live at Grandma's.

"Ma Hilly tell Mammie that Mattie and Abraham can help her in the land, cause since Pappy dead, she been neglectin' the land."

Jessica had to admit to herself that Grandma had a point there. Ever since she could remember, they would get to the few fruit trees Grandma owned, right after someone had just helped themselves to all the ripe fruit. Grandma would be hurt and angry.

"Dese people have no heart," she would exclaim. "Dey see a poor ol' lady, who husband dead, who only daughter dead, tryin' to raise her granddaughter an' dey jus' takin' advantage." Jessica would feel helpless and sorry for Grandma. So grudgingly, she had to admit that it might not be a bad idea for Aunt Mattie and Abraham to join the household after all.

CHAPTER 3

Not until her second year, did Jessica finally begin to relax and appreciate the experience of being in high school. She wasn't sure whether this change resulted because her friend, Madge, having won a scholarship to high school the following year, started attending the convent and she finally had a soul buddy or because she was eventually getting used to the school. As expected, she was an eager student. She enjoyed the new subjects she was being taught, especially English literature and biology.

At first, she was intimidated by the nuns in their strange habits which made their bosoms appear flattened. She and Madge discussed at length whether they were truly women.

"You think they have 'Susie' every month like real women?" Madge wondered.

"I don't think so," answered Jessica. "They probably old women and old women don't get 'Susie'." The truth was that she found it hard to think of these nuns in feminine terms.

It seemed the school was full of rules. There were bells and ranks and prefects to get used to. Not to mention frequent episodes of scolding and disciplining.

When the loud bell rang, each student had to make her way quickly into ranks. At the sound of the tinkle bell, students were supposed to become completely quiet. Zealous prefects stood by, with notebook and pen poised, to enforce these rules.

The fact that she won a scholarship - was an exhibitioner - as the nuns put it, was no longer a source of pride to Jessica. In fact, she felt more like a charity case. Many exhibitioners from poor families, traveled back and forth to their country homes every day. Unlike Jessica, who lived in the town, and could stay up late at night studying with the aid of electric light, many of these girls had to study by the flickering light of a candle or lamp. On arriving at school sometimes a uniform was not as crisp as should be because of the crowded bus ride or an assignment not completed. At these times the poor individual was sure to hear the dreaded comment from a nun "and she's an exhibitioner!"

It was at the convent that Jessica discovered she had a new title. She was illegitimate - her father and mother never married. Initially this was secretly a source of shame to her. She pretended that her parents were indeed married before her mother's untimely passing. When she realized that more than half of her classmates were illegitimate, she was happy to drop the farce. In the daily religious and scripture periods, the nuns spoke at length of the evil of 'sins of the flesh' and illegitimacy and how it was corrupting the society. She learned all about venial and mortal sins and took pains to make her nine first Fridays. She went to church and communion for the first Friday of nine consecutive months, to guarantee her place in heaven.

Jessica did not participate in extracurricular school activities. Perhaps it was because she preferred the sanctuary of her bedroom or maybe she felt that she didn't fit the mold that the nuns seemed to prefer for their concerts and extravaganzas. Perhaps she felt more needed at home. On a few occasions she visited the public library; but in spite of shelves packed with books, she could hardly find anything relevant and interesting to read. Even when she did the books presented a distorted account of the origins of her people. A book of Africa, portraying primitive women in the market place, clothed only in a loin cloth, helped to mislead her into feeling gratitude for the slave trade. It seemed that the slave trade had removed her ancestors from such uncivilized life.

Just before the end of Jessica's first school year, Albertine gave birth to Trevor and was laid up for several months with complications. During this period Jessica took over many of the household responsibilities. She did the cooking, cleaned the house, as well as took care of her sister, Debbie. She enjoyed reading to her little sister and taking her for walks some evenings, with her baby brother in his pram. Her father spent every day except Sundays in the store, where he worked long hours. What a relief to him that Jessica handled the household easily and efficiently. On that point, Albertine remained silent. She didn't complain, but neither did she acknowledge Jessica's assistance.

During her first few years in St. George's, Jessica returned to Rockville every Saturday night and took the bus back into the town before school started on Mondays. She told herself that she did this to keep her grandmother company. They attended Sunday mass together. Grandma loved to get dressed up in her

Sunday dress and hat. They usually sat towards the back of the church as the front half was reserved for those who paid pew rentals. Grandma had a beautiful alto and singing along with the choir was one of her favorite pastimes. After Mass, they invariably stopped to chat with many of the village folk, answering inquiries about how Jessica was getting along in school. Later at home they would sit on the verandah, in the cool shade of the flamboyant tree to have a breakfast of cocoa tea with johnny bakes and saltfish souse.

Jessica always brought a bag of her dirty clothes to be laundered, but Grandma wouldn't allow her to wash and iron clothes on a Sunday.

"You have to rest on de Lord's day chile," she would say. "Just leave de clothes dey." But then Grandma always washed and ironed Jessica's clothes during the week. The white blouses were bleached and starched and, using heavy irons on a coal pot, Grandma smoothed them to perfection. Jessica always had a clean bag of clothes to take back to town with her.

She sometimes visited the Baileys. She enjoyed sitting in the kitchen and talking to Ma Bailey, who was usually stirring a huge pot on the fireplace, with a large wooden spoon. Her apron, covering a wide expanse of tummy, was splattered with various food stains. After a while, Mrs. Bailey would put down her wooden spoon, wipe her hands in her apron and give her full attention to Jessica.

"Ah hope you keep doin' good in school, Darlin'," she always encouraged Jessica in a kind tone, a wide smile flashing across her dimpled cheeks. She was a short, round, 'hugable' woman. "Yoh grandmother so proud o' you."

Jessica never failed to talk to Jacob, Mrs. Bailey's twenty year old son, who sat in a corner of the kitchen, helping his mother shell peas or pound corn or simply scribbling his ABCs on a slate. Jacob was born with Down's Syndrome and perhaps because of this, his mother had a special place in her heart for him. For as long as Jessica knew herself, Mr. Bailey worked on an ocean liner and came home only once in a blue moon. Sometimes Madge and Flo came up the hill to visit Jessica and they would all sit on the verandah with Grandma and chat, occasionally getting a whiff of delicious smells from the kitchen.

On one of her visits to Rockville, Jessica discovered that Aunt Mattie and Abraham had moved into the back room, which used to be Grandma's room. Grandma had moved her bed and trunk into Jessica's room - the larger of the two bedrooms. Jessica was relieved because she had secretly feared the newcomers would usurp her space.

"So when you going to register for school?" Jessica asked Abraham, as he sprawled off on the verandah, one Sunday afternoon. Jessica noticed that while Aunt Mattie was constantly busy working the land - picking up cocoa and nutmeg - or washing and ironing, Abraham did little else but lay around the house all day long.

"I already finish standard VI...it doh make sense goin' back to school," he replied.

"You could finish standards VII and VIII and then get your school leaving certificate," offered Jessica. Abraham frowned. "First ah like smart arse people tellin' me what ah could do," he snarled.

"Sorry...sorry," said Jessica holding up both her hands. "Didn't mean to get your goat up." She told herself that henceforth she would say as little as possible to this idiot.

****

"You don't have to take de children walkin' no more," Albertine said to Jessica. "I'm dey mother and I should be de one to do dat."

"Fine with me," answered Jessica. She noticed that in the last month Albertine had been showing signs of improvement. The colour had gradually returned to her face. Last week she spent a few hours at the store. The day before Albertine was sitting in the verandah with Debbie and Trevor when Jessica returned from the convent. Albertine witnessed the gusto with which Debbie greeted Jessica.

"Jessica!" Debbie shouted, running towards Jessica throwing chubby, little, brown arms around her. "Let's go for walk now."

"Debbie," her mother said sternly. "Come back here...Jessica have to cook an' den clean out de kitchen."

"But I want Jessica to take me walkin'!" Debbie was at the point of tears.

"Don't worry Deb...we'll go as soon as I'm done," said Jessica, not understanding why Albertine was scowling at her. Daddy had complimented her on spending so much time with Debbie and keeping her clean and happy. "You're a godsend," he'd said to her many times. Now what did she do or say, to have the queen scowling at her like this?

When Albertine announced that she wanted to take the children walking herself, Jessica did not at all mind. She'd relished the opportunity for some quiet time to get an early start on her homework. Fine with me, she repeated to herself. I wonder if she would also want to start bathing Debbie and combing her hair too…and perhaps she wouldn't want me doing all this housework anymore. Jessica smiled to herself. I somehow doubt that, she thought.

That afternoon, while Albertine took the children walking, Jessica was sitting out on the verandah with her Latin book memorizing a list of verbs that were given for homework, when she heard a male voice call to her.

"Hi…Jessica."
She looked up to see the fellow next door, waving at her through his bedroom window. She knew his name was Jack DeCoutreau. He went to the Assumption college, which was the boy's high school, situated on the hill just above the convent. Apart from being a six footer with a gorgeous physique that no school uniform could hide, he was a great soccer player - the dream of many of her classmates.

"Hi," she answered shyly. She'd seen him many times but had no idea that he even knew her name.

"What you doin'…is dat home work?"

"Yes…Latin" she replied, hating herself for sounding so silly.

"Why you don't come watch the soccer game in the park tomorrow?"

"You playin'?"

"Of course." He didn't add "what a stupid question" but she felt it was implied. "So you gwine come?" he asked again.

"I'll see…" How could she tell him of all the housework she had to rush home to do - but maybe now that her stepmother was feeling much better, she wouldn't be needed that much at home anymore.

Before she saw them, she heard the screams of Debbie, and the wailing of the baby. She didn't want to antagonize Albertine further, so she waved Goodbye to Jack, with a tentative smile, and hastened indoors.

"Dis chile won' listen to me at all," complained Albertine to Jessica, as she came up the stairs breathlessly. With one hand she held on to Debbie, while supporting Trevor on her hip with her other arm, after lifting him out of his pram downstairs. "Since I sick, she get real spoil." Albertine went on. "You know she almost dash out in de road wid car comin'!"

Jessica frowned at Albertine. She felt this was a condemnation of her efforts in the household. Yes, since you get sick everything gone to pieces around here, she thought sarcastically. Debbie continued screaming, and tried to lurch towards Jessica, but was stopped by her mother.

"Go sit in dat chair in de corner," Albertine ordered her, pointing out the 'punishment chair' in the corner of the room. Jessica noticed the beads of sweat on Albertine's forehead. Frazzled from the incessant squealing of the baby, Albertine said to Jessica "Here…you take Trevor an' change him for me…leh me deal wid Debbie."
You don't have any *Please* in your mouth, Jessica thought, as she took the baby from Albertine and quickly replaced his wet diaper with a clean one and fresh camisole. She hurried to get him a bottle. The baby gave two little sighs before he hungrily took his bottle, and fell fast asleep in her arms.

With her mother promising a sweetie, if she would be a good girl and stop the noise, Debbie's screams soon changed to cries, which gave way to sniffles, which then stopped altogether. By then Albertine was complaining of a splitting headache. She left Jessica to give Debbie a bath and put her to bed. She went to her bedroom and collapsed on her own bed - a cold towel on her forehead.

The next day after she had done her chores, Jessica sat on the verandah, her biology book as a prop, secretly hoping she would spot Jack next door. There was no sign of him. The thought of knocking at his door crossed her mind but she quickly gave up that idea. Neither was there any sign from Albertine that she was planning to take the children for a walk again. *Maybe I should offer to take them.* But remembering Albertine's scowling face yesterday, Jessica decided to leave well alone. *Perhaps I'll just walk over to the park.* Jessica sauntered into her bedroom to spruce up herself to go out, but then she changed her mind again. Jack probably asked a million girls to come watch him play. *No, I think I'll just stay here away from the crowds.*

CHAPTER 4

Aunt Mattie was nothing like Grandma. She was slim while Grandma was buxom. Even though she was the much younger of the two sisters she was as frumpy as Grandma was elegant. She seemed to be in the same ill fitting, long, brown dress and old straw hat every time Jessica went home to visit. It was what she used when picking cocoa and nutmeg or working in the kitchen garden, which is where she spent most of her time. It was what she wore when she relaxed in the rocking chair on the verandah, while smoking her pipe or humming in an off key tone, late in the evenings. That outfit was like a uniform. Jessica was not at all surprised that it didn't take her long to earn the nickname, Scarecrow, in the Rockville community.

Abraham, on the other hand, was always properly groomed. His mother made sure that his clothes were neatly laundered and darned. He was a big fellow, who could 'inhale' a huge plate of food in seconds. Soon everyone started calling him Shark. After a while, perhaps only his mother remembered that his real name was Abraham.

"I don' know why you have dat boy like he some king," Grandma said to Aunt Mattie one Sunday afternoon. They had just finished a hearty Sunday dinner prepared by both Grandma and Jessica. While the women cleaned up the kitchen, Shark got dressed in his blue tennis shirt and blue shorts and went down the road. "You keep wipin' he backside for him all de time."

For months now it was obvious to Jessica that there was some tension between Aunt Mattie and Grandma. She guessed it had something to do with Shark and now she knew she was right. Aunt Mattie suffered from arthritis yet went to work in the land every day, with no help from Shark. She looked after the chickens too. She spent hours pounding cocoa with a mortar pestle to make cocoa balls, which she sold on Saturdays along with eggs and vegetables from the kitchen garden. It maddened Grandma that Shark did not lift a finger to help his mother. Aunt Mattie pursed her lips.

"You know hard work not for he, Hilda...so what you complainin' bout."

"Nonsense Mattie! What you mean hard work not for he? Jus' like you let dat wort'less Dawson crap all over you, so you lettin' Shark take advantage of you too."

"But you know Abraham is a delicate chile," Aunt Mattie insisted. Jessica gasped. Who was delicate... Shark? The same Shark who just consumed half a pot of 'oil down' and was now probably at *Percy's Rum Shop*, washing it down with some 'Jack iron'? Aunt Mattie had to be stark, staring mad to think so.

"Look yoh hands, Mattie...you need help," said Grandma in a pitiful voice, shaking her head in frustration.

"I doin' jus' fine," replied Aunt Mattie.

"Lord help us." Grandma threw her eyes and hands heavenward.

Jessica was baffled. She sensed a stubborn streak in Aunt Mattie yet felt pity for this poor woman, who had spent most of her life slaving after her ungrateful husband. According to Grandma, Mattie lost six children through miscarriages and still births before she finally surprised herself and everyone else by giving birth to a perfectly healthy baby boy late in life. No wonder she pampered him so much, thought Jessica.

Madge, who got her information from eavesdropping on conversations between her mother and Grandma, filled in some of the blanks for Jessica. She related that Aunt Mattie had encouraged her husband to go to England. She'd heard that it was easy to find good jobs there. She looked at the success of her best friend, Pearlie. Every single year since Pearlie's husband went to England he sent back a barrel full of goodies for the family. He sent them clothes and shoes and household products and canned foods. Sometimes he even included gifts for the neighbours. There were regular money orders in the mail as well. Aunt Mattie was so envious of her friend, that she was willing to sell the small portion of land they owned to 'make the passage money' for Dawson to go to England too. The plan was that he would get a job, find suitable accommodation and then send for her and Shark to join him.

Grandma said that Aunt Mattie got two letters from Dawson after he left Grenada. "One when he reach in England and six months later she get another one tellin' her he din find no job yet and to sen' him de rest o' de money from sellin' de land, as it gettin' real cold and he have to buy winter coat an' stuff." Grandma folded her arms and shook her head before she continued. "When she tell me dis damn nonsense, I tell her not to send de man any more money an jus' let his arse freeze. Pearlie done tell me her husband say Dawson move in wid some woman long time. I know Mattie wastin' her time on de ol' scamp."

"She send him more money?" Jessica asked Grandma.

"I t'ink she clean out her savings for dat scamp."

So it seemed that poor Aunt Mattie had waited and waited in vain to hear from her husband. Her letters were returned unopened. The years went by. What little money she was able to earn by doing day's work for the more fortunate, she spent on her son. Abraham was bent on keeping up the façade. He would tell his friends "Me fader have ah big job in England an' next year he sendin' for me to go live wid him."

The next year and the year after that would come and go and poor Abraham was still in Gauvine. His friends began to tease him. He grew ill tempered and sullen. His absences at school became more frequent, and when he did show up he would get into fist fights with other children. Finally Aunt Mattie decided to swallow her pride and agreed to accept her sister's offer to go live with her in Rockville. The change would be good for Abraham, she thought.

On Sundays, unlike Grandma, Aunt Mattie showed no interest in going to church. If she wasn't doing one of a thousand tasks, she would sit on the verandah, in the rocking chair, with her pipe. Neither did she care to socialize with the villagers, especially Mrs. Bailey whom she avoided like the plague. If Mrs. Bailey happened to come by, Aunt Mattie would invariably find some task to do down in the land or in the fowl coop.

Jessica noticed that occasionally, even when Shark wasn't at home, there was a faint whiff of strong rum, as she passed the back room. She wasn't sure if this smell came from Shark's clothes…or, she wondered, was Aunt Mattie secretly 'throwing back one' herself?

"I gwine make you a nice frock to go to church wid Mattie," Grandma told her sister one day. She recalled the old days when they both attended church frequently. Suspecting that the lack of proper apparel may be part of the reason Aunt Mattie chose to stay at home instead of going to mass on Sundays, Grandma thought she could easily rectify that. She consulted with Fleurina, who brought her some material from *Best Bargains*. Aunt Mattie stubbornly refused, insisting that Grandma make a shirt for Abraham instead.

"But Shark doh need no more shirt…de whole room full up wid his clothes" Grandma insisted but Aunt Mattie remained firm. Finally, Grandma gave up the idea altogether.

****

As the years went by, life at Willow Lane did not improve for Jessica but neither did it worsen. She liked the fact that Albertine spent a lot of time at the store, 'out of her hair'. At seven o'clock each morning Albertine opened the store which at that time of the day did a thriving business selling bread, eggs, milk and other dairy products. Ian joined her in the late morning and stayed until the store closed at nine p.m. Fleurina worked from nine a.m. to four in the afternoon, although many times she took work home with her. While both Flo and Ian were in the store, Albertine took the opportunity to spend a few hours at home. In those months when it was high season for tourists, she went to the hotels to drum up some business, before going home. She did not return to the store until Jessica got home from school at four p.m. This way she was able to get by with only a part-time maid.

Jessica enjoyed taking care of her little sister and brother. Compared to housework at Grandma's, the housework at Willow Lane, where there was electricity and all those fancy appliances, was fun. In little or no time she would have the meal cooked, the kitchen cleaned, the children bathed and lots of time for her school work.

During those hours at home, Albertine made a point of taking the phone out to the verandah when talking to her friends. She wanted every passerby to see that even though their house was not as grand as others on Willow Lane, they nevertheless had items of class, like a phone. The DeCoutreaus next door were well off - having returned to the island full of Aruba money. Even though Mrs. DeCoutreau was not employed outside the home, she had two full time maids. Albertine knew she could not compete on that level, but she made sure everyone was aware that she had a floor polisher and a state of the art food blender. In fact, when they were not in use, all the kitchen appliances were positioned on a high shelf, with the light on them, so that they could be seen clearly from outside. Albertine didn't seem to mind having to climb on a chair each time she needed to use one of her appliances. Of late she had been trying to convince Ian that they should take a vacation in Barbados. She thought to herself, this would certainly make the neighbours green with envy.

"Look how hard we been workin'…we need a holiday."

"What about the store?' asked Ian.

"If we time it for around Easter next year, Jessica can help in de store…and for heaven sake…we gwine be gone only two weeks."

Ian agreed to think about it. He liked the fact that Albertine seemed to semi-acknowledge Jessica's contribution. Jessica had helped them out in the store many a' time. Sometimes she brought the children along, allowing them to play in the back room, while she attended to customers in the front. Yes, it was doable. The idea gradually began to appeal to him. Certainly the store could be closed for two weeks at five p.m. each day.

Fleurina overheard these discussions and sure enough they were relayed to Jessica through Madge. Jessica relished the idea of two full weeks without the queen around. One reason was Jack. Recently, Jack had been a frequent evening visitor while Jessica did her chores or tried to study and take care of both Debbie and Trevor. He always timed his departure well before Albertine and Ian returned home.

Jessica finally got to see Jack play a game of soccer. The game coincided with Albertine taking the children to the annual church fair. Jessica was elated. Jack played the 'forward' position and to her amazement and his pleasure scored the winning goal of the game. The onlookers cheered loudly, while his team mates hoisted him aloft. He was the man of the moment. On the walk home after the game, Jack was swarmed by a group of young people, who had come out to watch the game and who wanted to bask in his glory.

"You see dat master shot Jack make," said a short, light-skinned girl in the group. Jessica thought her name was Louisa.

"Ah well" said Jack, with a no-big-deal toss of his head, reveling in all the attention he was receiving.

"De ball went zoom right into de net," continued Louisa enthusiastically.

"Pas' two defenders an' goalie an' none a' dem could a' stop it," another person added.

Jessica walked quietly at the edge of this group. There was no point adding her two penny bit, he was getting enough adulation already. When she eventually got to her gate, she waved goodbye to Jack and the others. Louisa was still there, even though Jessica was sure she lived on the street before Willow Lane that they just passed.

Jack flunked out of Assumption college two years ago, but that didn't matter, since he easily secured one of the more coveted employment positions in the town. He was a teller at the Royal Bank. The name 'DeCoutreau' was definitely the key that opened doors. With hair always neatly groomed and dressed in the latest style, showing off his athletic build, he was the object of many a secret and admiring glance. If Jessica thought he was adorable in his fancy work clothes, he was definitely irresistible in his soccer gear. Although he seemed to be showing a fair amount of interest in her recently, she was surprised when he invited her to attend the upcoming Old Year's Night dance with him.

"What you think I should wear?" she asked Madge and Flo, as they sat together on Grandma's mahogany bed.

"This" said Madge, holding up a puffed sleeved, red, peau de soie dress cut low at the neck and decorated at the top with sequins. Grandma had made that dress for Jessica last Christmas and it was the only fancy outfit she owned. But Fleurina, who was considered the expert on style, disagreed.

"You need somethin' wid a little more flash dan dat." She took out a sample of fabric from her purse. It was a crinkled lycra material of black and off-white. Jessica liked it instantly, especially when Flo described how easy it was to make a form fitting dress in that material. She was sold.

"It expensive…it goin' for $3.50 a yard but you only need a yard and a bit since the material so wide" Flo added, measuring Jessica from her shoulder to her knee. Jessica agreed to purchase the material.

"Good. I gwine bring it home next week."

During the next few weeks, whenever they had some spare minutes together, Jessica and Madge worked on the new dress. When she finally tried on the completed dress, Jessica could not believe how pretty she looked, as she glanced at herself in the long mirror Fleurina kept behind the closet door.

"Here, try it on wid dese high heels," Fleurina suggested.

Jessica gasped. "Oh, I love it!" she exclaimed, and rushed to embrace Madge and Flo. She had never had something so beautiful before. The dress hugged her in just the right places, while accentuating her beautiful dark brown skin and shapely long legs.

"Careful dis dress don' put you an' Jack in big trouble nuh," Flo teased.

"Wish I was a fly on de wall," Madge laughed.

CHAPTER 5

It was Christmas day. Since school closed in the middle of December, Jessica worked at least six hours every day in the store. She started at three in the afternoon on most days and didn't leave until closing time at nine o' clock. The week leading up to Christmas was usually the busiest time of the year, both at home and at the store. Jessica washed windows and hung new curtains, polished floors and baked fruit cake and pound cake for Albertine's household. At times she was just plain exhausted. Fleurina, in the sewing section, was also swamped, and needed almost full-time assistance from her sister, Madge. This was the time of year that business peaked - not only from tourists but also from locals, going to parties and weddings.

Ian repaid Jessica by allowing her to take groceries from the store up to Grandma's. He also slipped her some money when his wife was not around to object. Jessica waited until Albertine was out of the store and packed a ham, powdered milk, rice, flour, sugar, butter and other groceries she knew Grandma could do well with during the Christmas period.

Jack gave her a lift up to Rockville with these groceries at mid-week.

"Come in and meet my grandmother," she said to Jack when they arrived. So they both lugged the heavy grocery bags from the car up the gap to Grandma's home and deposited them on the dining room table. Grandma was busy in the kitchen, but she came out to the living room to meet Jack.

"Hello Ma'am," Jack smiled as Jessica introduced him to Grandma.

"So you de young fellow dat takin' Jessica to de Old Year's Night dance?"

Jack nodded shyly. Jessica never realized till then what an imposing presence her grandmother had. Despite the fact that she was in her home duster, she was tall and majestic. Jessica secretly hoped that Aunt Mattie would not put in an appearance in her dirty brown dress and old straw hat now. She loved her aunt dearly but that would be too embarrassing.

"Make sure you treat her real good now…okay?"

"Of course," Jack replied his head slightly down. Was he being intimidated by Grandma?

"And thanks for helpin' Jessica bring up all dis stuff for me."

"No problem," Jack replied. He seemed tongue tied. Where was the sharp, debonair Jack of the soccer field? Jessica decided to come to his aid.

"Grandma, Jack's Dad is waiting for the car…so we can't stay…but I'll see you as early as I can on Christmas eve."

****

Jessica decided to get a little shut eye, before it was time to go to midnight mass with Grandma, on Christmas eve.

It seemed as though she had just fallen asleep, when Grandma was waking her up.

"Time for you to get up, Jess," said Grandma, shaking her gently. "I put some warm water in the ewer for you to use."

Jessica reluctantly got up, washed herself in the basin with water from the ewer in the corner of the room, and got dressed. Although Grandma had recently acquired running water in the back of the yard, where by adding a few sheets of galvanize, she had constructed a lean-to shower stall, there was still no running water inside the house.

Jessica was surprised to see Shark, dressed in a gray, flashy suit with matching tie, was also on his way to church. Once a year, either at Christmas or Easter, Shark would surprise everyone and go to church. Aunt Mattie was busy making drinks.

They arrived just before the last seats in the church were taken. Jessica was relieved, as she was still very tired and she knew Grandma was too. That poor lady had gotten down on her hands and knees that week to scrub and polish the living room floor. The church was jam packed. People were standing in the back, on the sides and also along the steps leading up to the choir loft.

Before the mass began, the choir, joined by the congregation, sang many Christmas carols. This was Jessica's favorite part. She threw back her head and along with Grandma sang loudly 'Glow…ow..ow..ow.. ow ..ow …ow..ow..ow..ow..ow..ri..ah..in excelsis de..e..o'. Eventually a procession of acolytes, followed by the officiating priest, entered from the sacristy. Everyone stood up. Jessica noticed that Julian, Madge's youngest brother, who was an acolyte in the procession, was carrying the pot with the incense. He had complained earlier that the older acolytes seeking prestige, always hogged these important items, especially on days like Christmas, leaving the younger boys nothing to carry. He was determined that that wouldn't happen tonight. When their eyes met, Jessica secretly gave Julian the thumbs up sign and he returned a one-eyed wink.

The sermon was the part Jessica dreaded most. She hoped that it wouldn't go on and on tonight, in her tired state, as that would surely put her to sleep. Father Patrick always reminded Jessica of a squirrel, probably because of his bright, bulging eyes and excitable demeanor. He began his sermon by welcoming everyone who came to mass that night, but reprimanded those who came only at Christmas time.

"You know the church is here all year round…not only at Christmas," he informed the once-a-yearers. He then began to speak of the Baby Jesus and the true meaning of Christmas. "It's all about family," he said. Then continued a little louder "Family means a married mother, married father and one or more children."

He stopped suddenly. His eyes seemed to want to escape from their sockets as he surveyed the congregation fiercely.

"Family doesn't mean one man having children with several different women." Nobody in the church was sleeping now. "Family doesn't mean a woman hopping around fornicating with one man and the next." He finished his sentence on a crescendo. He paused for a short while, but everyone knew that more blasting was coming. This pause was only for effect.

"And those of you who are shacking up…living in sin…I say to you…the devil is in bed with you!" The eye of the hurricane was definitely upon the congregation.

The priest was now shouting at the very top of his voice as he leaned forward in the pulpit. Everyone was at the edge of their seats. Jessica heard snickering coming from behind her. *I hope the priest doesn't come down here and slap this person.* He seemed in just the correct mood for such a confrontation. For the next thirty minutes the congregation was scowled at, shouted at, and screamed at about their wicked and sinful ways.

Despite the severe blasting of the sermon, at the end of the service, the organist struck up a lively Christmas carol which both the choir and congregation belted out, thus ending the service on a positive note.

After the mass, Jessica walked home with Grandma and the Baileys.

"I t'ink Father Patrick mus' a stop in too long at *Percy's* tonight," Lenox Bailey joked. Madge and Jessica giggled.

"Don' let yoh mother hear you say dat 'bout de priest, boy."

"Grandma neither," said Jessica with a smile. "Unless you want a whippin' this big Christmas mornin'."

It never failed to surprise Jessica how Grandma could transform her little shack into a palace at Christmas time. You could almost see your face in the beautifully polished floors. The good lace curtains, used only on special occasions, fluttered gaily in the breeze. On a starched, frilly doily on the center table in the living room, a vase of anthurium lilies freshly cut from the garden gave a festive ambiance to the room. The chair-cushions were newly covered. Jessica noticed that some of the broken wooden rails of the verandah had been replaced and painted. She enjoyed the pleasant smell of freshly cut grass in the front yard and admired the neatly trimmed hibiscus fence. It was a lot of work and Jessica felt sad that she had not been there to help.

Aunt Mattie, who for once was wearing a clean frock and had finally taken off her old straw hat, proudly displayed bottles of sorrel and ginger beer that she had made, as well as the pigeon peas, yams, dasheen and sweet potatoes that had come from the garden. She was in a festive mood that morning. "Come have a drink, nuh," she said to Fleurina, whom she ignored most of the time. She led Flo into the kitchen. "What you want?" she asked as she pointed proudly to the bottles of drinks on the kitchen shelf. Fleurina opted for a glass of sorrel, while Aunt Mattie helped herself to a drink from her own bedroom.

Jessica's only job was to kill the cock that Grandma had picked out for their Christmas dinner. She hated to admit it but that was the one and only job she absolutely dreaded.

"Come help me please," she begged Madge. Last night she had tried to get Shark to agree to help her but he had refused, saying he was too busy.
Madge helped her to tie up the rooster. Luckily it was a 'clean neck' fowl and they didn't have to pluck neck feathers. The excitable rooster cackled and squawked noisily, unnerving poor Jessica.

"Hurry up Jessica...de water boilin' already" Grandma called from the kitchen.
Okay...it's now or never. Jessica was getting more nervous by the minute but she got the cutlass and while Madge tried to anchor the fowl on a big stone in the back yard, she delivered a deadly blow to the cock's neck.

The headless fowl jumped splashing its blood all over the girls. Madge screamed and jumped. Jessica almost dropped the cutlass on her own foot as she jumped while the fowl rolled pass her and disappeared under the nearby cocoa trees.

"Whey it go?" Jessica asked. They had tried to follow the catapulting bird under the cocoa trees, but with the thickness of the fallen dried cocoa leaves, seemed to have lost its trail. Jessica was poking at the cocoa straw with a stick trying to find the dead cock, that was to be a big part of their Christmas dinner.

"I don't know," Madge replied, nervously looking around her from the safety of a large rock. Snakes loved to hide in cocoa straw and she did not relish being here at all. Just then they viewed Jacob sitting underneath a roof of cocoa branches, his pockets bulging with mangoes, while his mouth, face and hands were covered with the yellow flesh from the fruit.

"Come help us look for the cock I jus' kill, Jacob."

"Looook eeeee dey," stammered Jacob as he pointed to the bird a few feet from where he sat. Jessica was so relieved to find the fowl, she didn't stop to wonder why on earth Jacob was beneath the cocoa trees eating her grandmother's mangoes.

She gave the dead fowl to Grandma, who had come into the back yard to find out what was taking them so long.

"Y'all covered wid de fowl blood," Grandma exclaimed, while both Jessica and Madge tried to act nonchalantly. "Go wash up an' change off" she instructed them. But before going to do so, Jessica helped her grandmother to pluck the feathers from the fowl, remove its innards, cut it up into pieces and then season it with fresh herbs from the kitchen garden.

"Now go sit in de verandah and relax," advised Grandma.

After washing up in the backyard shower stall, and changing their bloodied clothes, Jessica and Madge joined Flo and Aunt Mattie on the verandah.

"What y'all drinkin'?" Aunt Mattie inquired of the newcomers. Fleurina's glass was still half filled with sorrel, but Aunt Mattie's pan-cup was obviously empty.

"Sorrel," said Jessica.

"Ginger beer for me," Madge answered.

Aunt Mattie went to pour the drinks, at the same time helping herself generously to her own private drink which she seemed to keep in her back room. Back on the verandah, she continued the story she was telling Fleurina, while rocking back and forth on her rocking chair and every now and then helping herself to whatever was in her cup.

"I know dat was a sign...mih mamma use to say if you have a spill of milk while you makin' a baby..." Aunt Mattie took another swig from her pan-cup, before she continued. "Dat is a sure sign de chile gwine be delicate." Jessica noticed Madge and Flo exchange curious glances. *So that was where that ridiculous idea of Shark being delicate came from.* She felt embarrassed but sometimes Aunt Mattie awakened some protective instinct deep within her. She decided she would see to it that her aunt cut down on the drinking and maybe eat some thing salt. She was definitely at the 'plimsoll line' now. Jessica went into the kitchen and returned with a platter of ham sandwiches.

"Thank you," said both Flo and Madge, as they helped themselves, but Aunt Mattie declined.

"But I made it especially for you, Auntie...I want you to have it," Jessica insisted.

"Thanks Darlin' Doux Doux...you such a honey...but lemme put it up for Abraham."

Jessica felt herself getting annoyed. Where was Shark today? No one had seen him since the service last night. Was he down at *Percy's* again? Madge said he spent a lot of time with Miss Lucy recently. Wait till her husband finds out - he'll skin the brute alive. On Christmas day that bugger couldn't spend some time with his own mother?

"I put some up for him already," she lied. "This for you Auntie."

Aunt Mattie put her head back and drained the contents of her cup. "You know Abraham startin' nex' week to help Mr. Otway sell insurance," she announced proudly to the girls.

"That's good" said Jessica. *Shark working?...This I have to see.*

Aunt Mattie stood up with a "More drinks for anyone?"

"No thanks," they all answered together, as Jessica, putting one hand on Aunt Mattie's shoulder to get her to sit down again, gently took her cup away from her. "Let me put this down for you, Auntie."

"We should go help Mammie now," Flo and Madge both took that opportunity to make their exit, as Jessica, leaving Aunt Mattie with the plate of sandwiches on the verandah, returned the used wares to the kitchen.

"You know how many children I bury," Aunt Mattie said to Jessica as she returned to the verandah.

"Smell that chicken!" Jessica tried to steer the conversation to a more pleasant subject. "Hhhmmmm" she sniffed appreciatively at the aroma coming from the kitchen.

"I bury de las' baby gyurl below de dwarf coconut tree," continued Aunt Mattie, completely ignoring Jessica's comments. She rocked back and forth in her chair. "Dawson didn't want to christen any of de children... he say it ain't necessary..."
Jessica could see signs of tears in Aunt Mattie's eyes now. She held Aunt Mattie's hands in her own.
"When I git pregnant wid Abraham, I decide I not gwine tell him nuttin' but I gwine christen de baby."
Jessica wiped her aunt's tears away with her index finger.
"An' dat is de only chile dat survive...after I done lose six o'dem." The tears flowed freely now. Although these events happened thirty, perhaps forty years ago, it was obviously buried deep in her psyche - she couldn't let go of it.
Jessica put her arms around the old lady.
"If ah did know, Jessie...if ah did only know," she wept.
Jessica heard footsteps behind her and turned around to see Grandma standing behind them. She pulled up a chair and sat down. Jessica released Aunt Mattie.
"You know life not easy for nobody," said Grandma. "Everybody have dey own problem." Aunt Mattie sniffed. Grandma continued. "But everybody got a blessin' too and dey mus' appreciate dat." Aunt Mattie looked around her - perhaps for her pan-cup. "When Pappy fall off dat roof an' get kill, me heart almos' explode...I din t'ink I could a' go on. An' den Audrey get sick. I had to watch me poor chile come to skin an' bone. Lord!!" Grandma had a sad look in her eyes, as she recalled those difficult times. Jessica could never find out from her grandmother what ailment her mother died

from, so she was all ears - maybe now she would finally learn this big secret. She knew that her grandfather, Pappy, while working for one of the wealthy merchants in the town, had fallen off from a roof. Apparently the ladder, which wasn't secured properly, had slipped. A month's wages was all Grandma got in compensation for her husband's accident and death.

"But you know," said Grandma in a cheerier voice, "God take Audrey but give me Jessica…me lovely grand here, dat I so proud of." She rose from her chair and pulled Jessica to her in a bear hug. Jessica pulled up Aunt Mattie from her rocking chair, despite her protests, and included her in their embrace. They rocked around in a circle, holding on to one another.

"Mattie girl," said Grandma, "leh we take dat lemon life give us and make some good lemonade." A flicker of a smile passed across Aunt Mattie's weathered face.

****

Jessica looked astounding when she got dressed up to go to the Old Year's Night party with Jack.

"Oooh look at Jess," said little Trevor, pulling his mother by the hand so she could see how pretty Jessica looked. Jessica was secretly hoping that she would be gone before Albertine could glimpse her. After returning from the store on most nights, her stepmother and father stayed downstairs in the dining room listening to the radio. They did not come upstairs until bedtime. She had obtained her father's permission to go to the dance with a friend. There was no need to say anything to the queen.

When Albertine saw Jessica she was clearly surprised. When did that black, skinny, picky-head child that had come to live with them a few years ago become transformed into this beautiful, shapely, young lady? But instead of commenting favorably, she scowled and asked "Yoh take dat material from *Best Bargains?"* Jessica hesitated with an answer. She was beginning to formulate a suitable response, when there was a knock at the living room door. She slipped on Fleurina's black high heels, grabbed Madge's purse and hurried to the door.

As expected, it was Jack looking as dapper as ever in his new dandy suit. They smiled happily at each other. "Bye…I'm off," Jessica shouted loudly enough, so her father who was downstairs, could hear her. At the same time she waved goodbye in the direction of Albertine and Trevor, before discreetly shutting the door behind her. As she slipped in beside Jack in his father's *Morris Minor*, she glimpsed Albertine peeping at them through the jalousies. Oh well, now she knows who's taking me to the dance, thought Jessica.

The dance was a blast. The band played beautifully. Jessica couldn't believe the electricity she felt when Jack held her in his arms during the slow dances. Her knees felt weak. *Oh my God, let me not faint*, but she felt herself floating as if in the clouds and much too soon the set was over. She loved the fast pieces too. She finally got to strut her stuff as she often did in the Bailey's living room or on Grandma's verandah.

"Where you learn these moves, girl?" Jack was visibly impressed.

"You want some more?" she giggled mischievously.

After the dance, before Jack brought Jessica home, he parked the car on Labelle hill over looking the carenage. With the beautiful view of the St. George's harbour beneath them, he presented her with a little gift. It was wrapped in gold metallic paper with beautiful silver metallic ribbon.

"A Christmas gift for me?" asked Jessica surprised. When he had made a left instead of right turn at Panoramic road, she had wondered where on earth was he taking her.

"No...not a Christmas gift...Christmas is only one day in the year...this is forever."
Jessica was glad she was sitting down.

"Open it" he prompted, with a big smile on his face. This fellow is indeed romantic, she thought, enjoying every minute of it. It was a beautiful gold bracelet at the front of which was a heart encircling the letter J. She was shocked.

"Oh my God! It's sooo beautiful," said Jessica almost in tears.

"I designed it myself and got a jeweler friend of my Dad to make it," said Jack, pleased with her reaction.

"Is that me trapped in your heart?" She couldn't believe Jack had gone to all that trouble and expense for her.

"Yes...you are trapped in my heart...forever" replied Jack, as he pulled her gently towards him.

CHAPTER 6

"Shark actually lookin' good these days" Jessica observed to her grandmother. Since he started working for Mr. Otway, selling insurance, he had spruced up his appearance. Instead of rubber sandals and hairy legs sticking out of shorts, his new garb consisted of meticulously ironed long pants with cotton shirt and tie. His mother polished and shone his leather shoes to perfection every day. Shark was like a new person.

"I hope he gwine give his mother a little bit o' the money he makin'," replied Grandma.
Jessica saw Aunt Mattie's adoring eyes follow Shark down the hill to the bus stop. At least he didn't spend so much time anymore at *Percy's* or at Miss Lucy's place, she thought.

"Now he want egg every mornin' for breakfast an' guess what...he not eatin' saltfish and breadfruit anymore," Grandma continued to Jessica.

"Whaat?"

"I had to put me foot down...I tell him if is egg he want, he got to pay for it."

"And what he say?"

"His stupid mother jump in an' say since she is de one takin' care o' de fowls and sellin' de eggs for me, she gwine take her payment in eggs for Shark." Grandma sighed heavily. Jessica knew she had stepped on her grandmother's 'corn toe'. "Like father…like son" Grandma continued. "Bot' a' dem damn wort'less."

Jessica wanted to put in a good word for Shark and to say to Grandma, at least he's working now, but she decided to give Shark more time at this job, before she started speaking up for him.

****

"That Albertine is a real witch," Madge said to Jessica as they walked up the hill to the convent.

"What make you say that?" inquired Jessica. That was certainly no news to Jessica, but she was surprised to hear it coming so vehemently from Madge.

"Flo heard her tellin' Jack yesterday that you not good enough for him. She tell him he should find himself a nice light-skin or brown-skin girl, with good hair… you too black and low class for him."

"What?" Jessica was astounded. She knew she was not Albertine's cup of tea, but she never thought Albertine would stoop to do something as underhanded as this.

"After you spend the whole of the Easter holidays minding her children and helping out in the store…that's the thanks you get."

Jessica shook her head. "It's been a rough five years, but the end almost here."

"I hope you don't *'peter'* on that witch after you leave there," said Madge. She was even more angry than Jessica. She couldn't understand why Flo hadn't spoken up for Jessica, since she was right there, when that conversation occurred. "That's just not right."

"As Grandma always says," Jessica said softly "every pig have a Saturday."

In less than three weeks, Jessica was going to be writing her O Level exams. She had been able to keep at the top of her class for the past few years. She was glad that Jack was going to be touring the islands with the Grenada soccer team during exam time. He could be a real distraction sometimes. He didn't understand that she needed time to study. Since Easter, when Ian and Albertine went to Barbados and there was no father and stepmother to worry about, things had definitely heated up between them.

"I've found the person I want to spend my whole life with," Jessica confided in Madge dreamily.

"And he want to spen' his whole life with you?"

"Of course. Yesterday he swore that I was his one and only love...he always says I'm trapped in his heart forever." Madge was totally impressed.

"You so lucky Jess. When you goin' to bring him to meet Ma Hilly and the family?" she asked.

"I already introduced Jack to Grandma...they've met a few times."

"I mean when you goin' to bring him to sit down and meet with the *whole* family," Madge explained. She included the Baileys in 'whole family'. When Chester and Flo began a serious involvement, two years ago, Chester was invited to meet the 'whole family', which included Grandma and Jessica.

Jessica was slightly embarrassed. She hesitated to admit to Madge, even to herself that she didn't want Jack to see her Aunt Mattie smoking her pipe in her dirty frock, on the verandah. Not that he would love her any less, but the time was not right yet.

"Soon" she said to Madge. Then added "But he's real busy with soccer now."

Jessica was looking forward to her graduation at the beginning of July and dancing the graduation waltz with her fine, handsome love. Of course she would wear the beautiful, gold bracelet he had given her. It was the symbol of their undying love. And then she would be done with high school and Albertine forever.

"Albertine don't know it yet, but Flo leaving her next year," Madge continued.

Jessica knew that Flo was planning to get married to Chester Bain from Grandville that coming December, but she didn't realize that she was going to leave *Best Bargains*. Flo certainly enjoyed her work there and claimed Albertine paid her well and treated her fairly.

"Why?...she not gwine work after she get married?" asked Jessica.

"She and Chester leaving for England soon after," Madge informed her.

That was news to Jessica. She knew Flo's departure was going to hurt the business badly. Fleurina was reliable and methodical. At peak times she was able to do the impossible. Her work output was exceptional. Albertine was not stupid. She knew where her bread was buttered. She realized she could never replace Flo and did her best to keep her happy. But at this point Jessica didn't care.

"I can't imagine not having Flo around," muttered Jessica.

"I'm leaving too, as soon as I finish high school," said Madge.

****

Exams were finally over. Jessica thought she had done well. Now she felt exhausted. Even after she heard Albertine leave for work and knew she should get up to prepare the children's breakfast, for some strange reason she couldn't budge.

I'll just take ten more minutes, she said to herself. The next time she opened her eyes it was almost nine o' clock. *Oh my God...Debbie and Trevor going to be late for school!* Jessica hurried up from bed, threw on her duster and ran downstairs.

"Don't worry" said Ian, who was just returning from dropping off the children at school. "I gave them breakfast. You okay?" he asked, giving Jessica a concerned look. "You seemed so tired, I decided not to wake you."

"Thanks Daddy," answered Jessica. "I didn't realize how much these exams took out of me...but thank God...they're done now."

"Why you don't sit down and join me with some tea and bakes, before I go down to the store" Ian suggested. Jessica couldn't help but notice how different her father acted towards her when Albertine wasn't around.

"Sure...just let me brush my teeth first and I'll be right back."

After a few minutes, Jessica was back downstairs. Ian was busily checking the cricket news in the Trinidad newspaper. She poured two cups of tea, added milk and sugar to them and then joined her father at the table.

"The West Indies team going to play Pakistan tomorrow," he advised. "Then whoever win going to move on to play either England or Australia."

"Mmhmm" answered Jessica. This morning she just wasn't interested in cricket. She placed two little plates in front of each of them, and removing two of the bakes from a tray on the stove put one in each plate.

"Butter?" she said to her father, as she passed him the butter dish and knife. She wanted to ask him about her mother. She didn't want to talk about cricket now. Ever since she started going with Jack, she was curious as to why her mother had been only her father's 'side kick'. Did he ever consider getting married to her? If not - why not? This morning it seemed as though she had seen or dreamt of her mother again but this time there were tears in her eyes.

"What was Mummy like Dad?" she blurted out suddenly to Ian.

"Whaat?" Ian stammered, as he folded the newspaper. This ball had come at him out of left field, as the saying goes. "But yoh grandma have her picture."

"I mean…what was she like *to you*. Tell me about Mummy, Dad" Jessica leaned forward in her seat, looked at her father directly in his eyes as she emphasized 'to you'. She needed desperately to hear about her mother from her father's lips.

"You look like her, Jess. You have the same beautiful eyes like your mother." Jessica remained silent, still looking directly at him. After a while Ian continued. "And she was smart too, just like you." Ian took a slurp of his tea, put his cup down, then said to Jessica, "You a smart girl, Jess…don't ever let anybody tell you, you're not." He placed both his hands on the table as he hoisted himself up from his seat. Then in a low voice, almost to himself, he said "Audrey was a beautiful woman." Turning around to face Jessica who was looking up at him, he added "I didn't know that then...but I know it now."

****

Fleurina was secretly getting ready for two huge events in her life and being the highly organized individual that she was, she started her preparations right away.

"Please don't mention the wedding to a single soul," she cautioned Jessica and her siblings. "It's gwine be very small and the fewer people know about it, the easier it will be to keep it small."

"How many people you planning to invite?" asked Madge. She was disappointed that she couldn't publicize this good news all over Rockville and St. George's. Besides she was hoping that Flo wanted the usual entourage of bridesmaids and maid of honour - a part she was hoping would be hers.

"Just family and close friends," answered Flo.

"Well both you and Chester come from very big families...so it can't be dat small," said Madge.

"That's why I don't want a peep of this mentioned until I send out the invitations."

Jessica saw the plan. Poor Flo was hoping that her brother from Richmond with his wife and six children couldn't all possibly attend her wedding, with three months notice. The same went for her sister in Trinidad, who would need to be told at least a year in advance to transport the entire family of ten over for the wedding.

One of the first things on Fleurina's 'to do' list, was to get a passport. Chester already had his but since Flo had never left the island that was a document she never obtained. The clerk at the Passport office told her, she needed her Baptism or birth certificate and three 2x3 inch photographs.

Flo phoned the parish priest to obtain a copy of her Baptism certificate. Lo and behold she made the startling discovery that the girl child born to Ethel and Cyprian Bailey, bearing her correct date of birth, was not called Fleurina Anastasia Bailey, as she had been led to believe this past twenty five years, but Jane Elizabeth Bailey. Fleurina was definitely confused.

"What? There's something wrong here!" she exclaimed, when she opened the envelope with the document at home in her bedroom. "Mammie!" she called for her mother. Mrs. Bailey came in from the kitchen, drying her hands on her apron. She was just as confused as Flo. Then it came back to her.

"You know, when I carry you for Baptism, and I give de priest yoh name, he say dat not a saint name and you must have a saint name." Mrs. Bailey stopped for a while trying to remember the correct sequence of events, so long ago. "But me and Daddy insist. We tell de priest we want to call you Fleurina Anastasia and nuttin' else."

"Good," Fleurina nodded but there was still a big question mark on her face. Mrs. Bailey continued,

"He say okay we could call you whatever we want. I never did notice dat he still write Jane Elizabeth on de certificate." Mrs. Bailey was looking at the certificate as if it were a viper about to charge.

"All my school records have Fleurina on it," said Flo. Baptism or birth certificates were not a requirement for getting into schools in Grenada. "Everybody know me as either Flo or Fleurina. I not gwine change dat now."

"But what you going to use on your passport?" asked Jessica.

Flo frowned. "This is such a mess," she said annoyed.

"Jane Bailey…what a stupid sounding name," said Madge, pronouncing the name slowly and making a face.

"I think Jane Bain will sound even worse," said Jessica, referring to Chester's family name that Fleurina was about to change to.

"Maybe your name is not what we been calling you either," said Flo sharply to Madge. "You better go check it out."

Jessica wondered at the exotic names the girls in the Bailey family certainly had. Madge's full name was actually Madgrita and she recently discovered that the full names of Lisa and Terri - their two older sisters, were really Estrelisa and Terrantula. *Holy macaroni!* But how could there ever be a saint with the name Fleurina Anastasia, unless a human died and went to heaven? Wasn't that the process? Did saints only have names like Jane Elizabeth? She was totally confused.

CHAPTER 7

Jessica gradually began moving her belongings back to Grandma's. This was now officially her home again. She still remained partially at Willow Lane because Ian kept asking her to stay on to help in the store and at home. *Best Bargains* was undergoing a very busy period. Jessica agreed to help out until September, when she was to start teaching at *Our Lady of Fatima* catholic elementary school.

But something was bothering her. She couldn't remember the last time she had her period. She thought it was due sometime during her exams. When it didn't come she told herself she was simply stressed out. What with all that studying for exams, then the excitement of getting ready for graduation, then working hard at home and at the store, she had to be stressed out. She simply needed to relax. But even though she slept more, because she was always so tired, it didn't seem to help. Two weeks later, she was definitely worried.

Perhaps I'm just run down. Some multivitamins would certainly help. So she went down to the St. George's square, to get some multivitamins from the pharmacy. Before she approached the cash to pay for them, she noticed a sign advertising pregnancy test kits.

Three easy steps that you can do at home the sign said. *Perhaps I should try this.* She looked around and not seeing anyone in the store she knew, privately retrieved one of the kits. To throw the cashier off the scent, as they were always so nosy, she picked up a big box of sanitary napkins as well. She walked out of the store with her purchases and almost bumped right into Fleurina.

"Hey Jess."

"Hi Flo" Jessica was a bit unnerved. *One second more and she would have caught me buying this kit.* She quickly composed herself, smiled and said "you left work early today?"

"No...I jus' takin' a five...I have to go back."

In the bathroom, Jessica read the instructions for the test. Positive looks opaque like this - negative looks clear like that - and now the test. She stirred her urine around in the circle on the card, and within seconds it changed to opaque. *Maybe I did it wrong.* Jessica threw out the card, reread the instructions and repeated the test three times. Each time the result was the same - positive. She threw away the cards in the big garbage bin at the side of the house and went and lay down on her bed and sobbed. Her sobs gradually increased in intensity as her shoulders shook uncontrollably.

Oh my God! Oh my God...what to do? A million thoughts rushed through her head. Should she tell Jack? How would he react? Would his 'love forever' survive this? What was the name of the bush tea it was rumoured Miss Lucy took to get rid of her unwanted pregnancies? No -no - she couldn't do this. Madge would certainly know what to do - but she couldn't trust her best friend with this. Not just yet. She would definitely forfeit that job at the elementary school now. After all, it was a catholic school. She would disappoint so many people who were rooting for her. Grandma had sacrificed so much for her. Her father would be so disappointed. Jessica wept into her pillow.

****

"Why don't you stay down this weekend and go to Grand Anse with us on Sunday?" Ian asked Jessica. Most Sundays Ian took Debbie and Trevor for a swim at Grand Anse beach. Trevor boasted that his Dad said he could swim like a fish now. Debbie, on the other hand, wasn't at all interested in swimming but enjoyed going to the beach to show off her fancy swim suits. Her mother spoilt her with lots of different outfits and beautiful swim suits when she came back from her Barbados holiday. It was ages since Jessica herself had been to the beach and normally that would be a treat, but recently all she felt like doing was crawling into a hole and staying there.

"Who's going?" asked Jessica. These days she couldn't stand the sharp scrutiny of her grandmother, who watched her every mood. Last weekend she wanted to know why Jessica was so listless. Maybe she should remain at Willow Lane this weekend and go to the beach with her father - if and only if - the queen was not going too.

"Albertine going to get her hair done after Mass" answered Ian, as if reading her mind. "So it will be just the four of us."

Jessica was satisfied. Albertine had found a new hair stylist, who every week did her hair up in a Mahalia Jackson do. There was no way she was letting the tiniest salty spray from the water near her hair. Besides, Jessica hoped that if she remained at Willow Lane, she would get a chance to talk to Jack privately. She decided she was going to bite the bullet and tell him about the pregnancy.

"Jack" she called to him from the verandah, on Saturday morning, when she saw him coming down the side stairs from his home.
"Hi J...what's up?" Jack smiled.
"Can we go for ice cream this evening after I leave the store?"
"That'll be great...but you not going up to Rockville?" Jack asked surprised.
"No...not this weekend." Seeing the puzzled look on Jack's face, as she seldom spent Sundays at Willow Lane, unless there was a good reason, added "Daddy taking us to the beach tomorrow."
"Grand Anse?"
"Yes."
"Maybe I'll come down there tomorrow too," he smiled.

Jessica didn't go to the beach the next day. In fact after she got the picnic basket ready for Ian and the children to take to the beach, she went back to bed complaining of a terrible headache. She looked pale. Ian was worried about her. Trevor was disappointed.
"But you have to see my back stroke, Jess" he whined.
"Next time," she promised. He kissed her gently on the cheek. She was almost overwhelmed.
"You're such a sweetheart, Trev" she said as she hugged him. "I promise I'll come watch you swim another time."

The night before, after she had spoken to Jack, she walked home alone, her whole world in shambles. Was this how her mother had felt nineteen years ago, she wondered. She couldn't possibly go to the beach the next day and smile and laugh as if everything was okay. In fact she would be grateful if a bolt of lightning were to strike her dead now.

The following week, Jessica got through her chores and worked at the store on 'cruise control'. She felt like a robot. She filled her days with work. The harder she worked, the less time she had to think of her situation. She cooked, baked, cleaned, worked in the store and at night after Debbie was asleep, cried softly into her pillow.

****

Shark was strutting about Rockville like a big shot. He bought himself a leather briefcase and a pair of dark sun glasses, which he wore everywhere - even at night. The company was going to give him a car, he said. It was a good thing he got his friend at *Percy's* to teach him how to drive. There is no way you could get a job like this, if you didn't know how to handle a vehicle, he said proudly, as if 'handling a vehicle' was the most difficult thing in the whole wide world. Aunt Mattie nodded happily as each sentence fell like precious pearls from her son's lips.

"I always did know you had it in you, son" she said.

"Good for you," said Grandma. "The Lord know we could do wid some dollars 'round here."

"When I get de vehicle, I gwine give all o' y'all a ride in it," Shark said proudly, ignoring Grandma's remark while looking in Jessica's direction. She had not made a single comment about his good fortune yet.

"Will be nice," answered Jessica with a forced smile. She couldn't understand how selling insurance, in a place where most people were struggling to meet their day to day needs, could be so profitable. But she didn't want to rain on Shark's parade.

"An' in September, Jessica gwine be teaching at *Fatima's*," announced Grandma. "Mattie girl, de time soon come when me an' you could relax."
Jessica gulped. She felt she was standing at the edge of a precipice. All she had to do was jump - but she couldn't.

****

"How come you never tell me Jack going away to England?" Madge asked Jessica reproachfully. According to Flo, Mrs. DeCoutreau made this announcement at *Best Bargains* yesterday. They didn't want to say anything before, Mrs. DeCoutreau said, until the passage was confirmed and everything was set. Until he got settled, Jack was going to stay with her brother who had a house in London. Her brother was going to help him find a job. Madge was rambling away, when she turned to look at Jessica and saw the tears pouring down her cheeks.

"Don't cry, Jess" she said, putting an arm around Jessica. "You could go join him after a little while." Jessica's sobs grew louder.

"I have to go" Jessica said, and rubbing at her eyes, left the Bailey girls' bedroom and bounded up the hill to Grandma's house. My, she's taking Jack's going away badly, Madge thought.

She didn't help Grandma with the Sunday dinner that day. Instead, Jessica lay face down on the bed, weighted down by both a physical and an emotional anchor. She was rescued by sleep. Later that evening after Jessica picked at her supper noticeably, she quietly helped Grandma with the dishes, cleaned up the kitchen and went back to the bedroom. Grandma followed her to the bedroom wondering why Jessica had barely eaten and made the surprising discovery herself.

"Oh mih Lord, Jessie" she said, holding Jessica's chin with her right hand and moving her face from side to side, looked into her eyes. "You pregnant?!" It was a half question, half astonishing statement. Jessica wasn't sure what Grandma was seeing on her face or in her eyes to make this diagnosis. But Grandma was right on the button. Jessica held her head down and her eyes closed as the tears spilled out of them.

"Yes Grandma," she whispered. "It's true." She poured out everything to her grandmother. She told her what Jack had said to her, the night she informed him of the pregnancy. She felt an acute sense of relief, once she had 'spilled all the beans' to Grandma. She couldn't bear to carry this burden alone anymore. But she was aware of her grandmother's deep disappointment as she saw her shake her head sadly from side to side, quietly murmuring "Not again Lord…not again."

Grandma sat heavily down on the bed. Jessica sat on the floor, her head in her grandmother's lap. She was Grandma's shining light, her star, her hope, but now she had let both Grandma and herself down badly. Grandma stroked her hair gently.

"Jessica…first t'ing tomorrow morning, I want you to go see Dr. Miller in de clinic. Okay?"

"Yes Ma," Jessica replied meekly. She would have to go very early as there was usually a long line up. She didn't want to be late getting to *Best Bargains* for noon.

"And Sweetheart…whatever happen…we gwine deal wid it together…you not alone." Jessica never appreciated a kind word more. It was like balm on a wound. She got up, put her arms around her grandmother and hugged her.

"I'll make you proud of me again Grandma…I promise."

"I know you will," Grandma answered. Then taking Jessica's hands in her own callused ones, looking into her eyes, she continued "We all human, Jessica. When you make a mistake, you don' have to remain down. You have to get back up again and hold yoh head high."

asking Jack for Jessica. Where was Jessica? Why was she not at his important party?

"She couldn't make it," he told them. "She have big business with her grandmother in the country." He would shrug his shoulders as if to imply that's the way it was and he couldn't help it. Jessica was shocked to learn that Louisa was at the party and danced 'the last dance' with Jack. She heard the rumour that Louisa was going up to England soon.

"You have to forget dat boy," Grandma said to Jessica, observing the look of sadness in her granddaughter's eyes. "He's ah dawg…and what goes around comes around. Trust me Darlin'…every pig have a Saturday." Jessica never failed to be comforted by her grandmother's words of wisdom and support. Secretly, she had been thinking that Jack would eventually get over the shock - God knows it was a shock for her too - and he would at the very least contact her. Now she knew differently. All that business of her being trapped in his heart forever, was pure bull. *Grandma is right…I have to forget him and move on.*

Grandma didn't tell Jessica but she learned from Aunt Mattie that on two occasions Grandma rang the doorbell at the DeCoutreau's home. No one answered. Jessica was well aware of their habit of screening visitors by peeping through an upstairs window. Someone must have seen her and decided not to answer. After a half hour of waiting and ringing, Grandma left, but she didn't give up. After her second visit she walked over to the Royal Bank and looked for Jack at the booth. Unfortunately or fortunately for Jack, she was told by one of the tellers that he had resigned from his job the previous Friday.

****

Jessica was discreetly informed that the teaching position at *Fatima's* that was promised to her, was going to another candidate. Deep down she was expecting this, but nevertheless when it did happen it felt like another dagger in her heart.

"What am I to do now?" she worried. She couldn't possibly rely on poor Grandma for support any more. It was her turn now to carry the torch. She began helping her grandmother with the few sewing jobs she got, in the hope that this would bring in more work. Fleurina passed a lot of the work she brought home from *Best Bargains* to Jessica. It was a bit ironic - now that she no longer lived at Willow Lane - she actually got paid for this work. She helped in the kitchen garden and began making preserves that Aunt Mattie sold along with her other goods in the market place. It was amazing how much effort one had to extend for so little reward.

By a stroke of luck Jessica heard that Mrs. Gittens was looking for a math tutor for her daughter. Jessica immediately offered her services. Building on that idea, she advertised and got a steady flow of students - both elementary and high school. Grandma's small dining room, which was separated by a half wall from the living room, was used as a class room during this time. She tried to divide the children into groups. Six days a week she gave lessons. On Saturday mornings she helped two little boys from elementary school with their arithmetic and reading. Later she had a more advanced set from high school that she helped with their English and Spanish. She taught algebra and geometry to another group every evening after school. Her days were filled and so they passed quickly.

At the beginning of September, shortly after Jack left the island, the Cambridge O Level results were received. Not wanting to approach the convent in her 'shameful' condition, Jessica had Madge pick up her results and certificate. Together with Grandma and Aunt Mattie, they looked at her results. Jessica did very well. She got credits for every subject she'd written, with distinctions in English literature and biology. She was elated. She felt she could and would overcome any hurdles that confronted her. "I am strong…I'm invincible…I am woman" she sang out loudly as Madge and Grandma joined in. And this time she felt she really meant it. In fact weeks later, when she received not a single word of congratulations from her father and stepmother, although disappointed, she certainly wasn't crushed. Fleurina said Ian made a big point of showing the results that were posted in the daily newspaper, to everyone who came into the store.

****

Later that month, Fleurina sent out her wedding invitations and officially informed Ian and Albertine of her upcoming wedding in December. Albertine was displeased that they were not invited, not accepting Fleurina's explanation that she and Chester were having a very small wedding with family only, and not even all their family either. Actually the only reason Fleurina bothered to inform them this soon, was to ensure she got the time off that week between Christmas and New Year's.

CHAPTER 9

No one knew just why and how it happened, but Shark lost his job at the insurance company. He never got to 'handle the vehicle' as he had been promised. He regressed into a sullen and gloomy mood, which cast a dark shadow over the whole house on the hill. He didn't speak to anyone. He remained in his bed in the back room for the better part of the day, and resumed his visits to *Percy's* in the late evening, returning in the wee hours of the morning. Aunt Mattie was distraught. She took to spending most of the day down in the land, in the shaded darkness underneath the cocoa trees. Jessica tried to console her. She tried to use Aunt Mattie's own words back at her.

"You have to stand tall Auntie. Don't let it get you down." Aunt Mattie responded by smiling mirthlessly in her direction. Jessica saw evidence that she was slowly 'losing her marbles'.

Poor Grandma was worried about everyone. Although Shark's job had not helped the household financially, yet it had put a strut in his step and a sparkle in his mother's eye. For that it had been worth it. Now Mattie was pretending to be working underneath the cocoa, but Grandma knew exactly what was going on down there. She smelled the liquor each time Mattie came up from there. Mattie hadn't done a stroke in the kitchen garden nor fed the fowls in the coop this whole week. They could be dead for all she cared. Thank God for Jessica, who found time to help with these chores before her evening classes. But she worried that Jessica was working much too hard. She didn't care what that Dr. Miller said, Jessica was huge for seven months. She suspected twins. Grandma herself had had twin boys that never made it. She wanted Jessica to rest more - to give the babies the best chance she could.

"Girl, I think you put on ten pounds since yesterday" Madge teased Jessica, as they both sat on the verandah, chipping coconut to feed the fowls later. Grandma heard the comment and even though it was exaggerated, confirmed her belief that Jessica was having a twin birth.

"I can hardly see my feet anymore" Jessica laughed. Apart from gaining a lot of weight, Jessica didn't experience that bogged down, tired feeling any longer. In fact, now she had energy to spare. She was happy to be able to increase Grandma's little bank account, with the money she made from tutoring. They both spent a lot of time sewing baby chemises and diapers. Yesterday, Grandma bought even more material for diapers in spite of the fact that Jessica was convinced they already had more than enough.

"You settle on a name for him yet?" Madge had long decided that Jessica was carrying a boy.

"Not yet…but it's going to start with a J," Jessica answered. She wasn't quite sure why she wanted her baby to have a name starting with the letter J. It had something to do with that bracelet she got from Jack, which she kept hidden at the bottom of her suitcase, under her bed. She was going to give it to this baby, sometime in the future.

"Joseph, John, Jade, Jonathan..." Madge began rattling off a bunch of names, when Jessica changed the subject.

"Flo got the lace for the bridesmaids' dresses yet?" Jessica asked Madge.

Four of their nieces were to be bridesmaids and Madge had the position she always wanted as maid of honour. The small family wedding was turning out to be a much bigger affair than Fleurina and Chester intended. Their brother from Richmond with his family of six were all attending, as was her sister in Trinidad but with only her two youngest children.

"Yes...she got it from *Ruby's*."

"Not from *Best Bargains*?"

"No. Albertine kept forgetting to order it" Madge replied with a smirk. "I believe she vex that Flo didn't invite her to the wedding."

Just as they were finishing with the coconut, both Jessica and Madge turned their heads towards the backyard. A loud commotion was heard coming from down the hill. Grandma heard it too and hastened outside. Jessica got up and joined her grandmother, tilting her head to better hear the hubbub that was going on. Madge followed closely behind Jessica.

"He's a big t'ief!" They heard Aunt Mattie shout clearly. Who was she talking to? Then they heard Mrs. Bailey reply,

"If I was you Mattie...I won' bad-talk nobody chile like dat. You don' see dat nut you have dey...nuh?"

Jessica was trying to keep up with Madge and her grandmother who were now racing down the hill. As she got closer she saw Ma Bailey's arm around Jacob stooping down on the ground, his head between his knees. Aunt Mattie was waving a stick at both of them threateningly.

"You talkin' bout me son? Watch dat idiot boy you have dey. Okay? He nuttin' but ah t'iefin' tom cat," she yelled as Grandma caught up with her.

"Come now, Mattie" Grandma said, taking the stick away from her sister and leading her away firmly by the arm. Aunt Mattie was reeking of alcohol. She had no choice but to follow Grandma's lead. Mrs. Bailey shook her head in frustration and heavily shuffled inside.

"What happen Jacob?" Madge asked her brother as Jessica stood by. His face and hands were soiled with mango juice. Jessica had long ago discovered that one of Jacob's pastimes was to sit quietly underneath her grandmother's cocoa and feast on mangoes that had fallen from the tree. Finally looking up, he saw Madge and Jessica.

"Yooh waant?" he asked innocently, as he took out a half ripened mango from his pocket and with dirty hands held it towards them.

"You have it" said Jessica, patting his back.
 She went and sat with Mrs. Bailey in the kitchen for a while. She regretted the incident that had just occurred and wanted to make sure that Mrs. Bailey understood that. Soon she herself would be a mother. There was so much she could learn from this woman who had almost single-handedly raised a family of ten children, all with different needs, efficiencies and deficiencies, yet remained positive and smiling. At least most of the time she did.

****

Although they never spoke about it, both Ian and Albertine felt the effects of Jessica's absence. When Ian did the books at the end of the month, he discovered that they paid out considerably more for sewing than they did when she was there. At home, Albertine needed to hire a full time maid now. This was just for a short while, she assured Ian, not wishing to draw attention to the fact that with Jessica not being around, she now needed a full-time maid. Ian always claimed she used his daughter as a live-in maid. But four months later Ian noted the 'short while' hadn't passed yet.

The children definitely missed Jessica. Trevor never ceased to inquire about her. "When Jessie coming back?' he asked almost every day. At the beach, he said to his father as he swam up and down in the crystal clear water "I want Jessie to see me swim, Dad" or "Jessie promised to come see my back stroke." When Albertine combed Debbie's hair, Debbie complained that she didn't do it quite like Jessica. She tried side plaits or cornrows or ponytails with colourful bubbles, but it didn't seem to measure up. Eventually Albertine gave up in frustration. No matter how she tried, she was unable to erase Jessica's presence from her household.

Ian planned on getting in touch with Jessica, after the O Level results were out and he heard of her success. He was going to give her a nice sum of money. But it just got away from him. Having to go to the doctor in Trinidad about his problem consumed most of his time and he didn't get around to doing so. But Christmas was coming and he would definitely contact her then. He would bring up a load of groceries to the household and he was sure the money would be welcome whenever it arrived. Poor Jessica…Albertine had not treated her well, while she lived with them. He should have put his foot down in her defense more than he did. And that stuck up DeCoutreau boy, used her and broke her heart just like he himself did with her mother. Ian didn't want to think about that. He felt a pang of guilt. It was too late for him to do anything about Audrey now, but he was going to try his best with Jessica.

****

The day of the wedding was here. It was even more gorgeous and sunny than Flo and Chester had dared to hope. Jessica opted to play a very low keyed behind-the-scenes role. She was not going to the church nor to the reception at the Bailey's home. Grandma was getting dressed for the wedding in the bedroom. She hummed happily to herself. It was a good month for her as a seamstress. She sewed several of the outfits for the occasion.

For the better part of the day Jessica was pressing and styling hair with a hot comb and curler, which she borrowed from Fleurina. She did Grandma's, Madge's and a couple of the bridesmaids'. Yesterday both she and Grandma cooked and baked for the wedding. She didn't complain but her legs and back ached. So she was resting quietly on the verandah now.

"How I look?" asked Grandma, stepping out onto the verandah in a green taffeta dress with green and white wide rimmed hat, white shoes and handbag.

"Nice," said Jessica admiringly, "but let me give you a little lipstick and makeup." She hoisted herself heavily from the chair and waddled back inside behind Grandma.

"That's better," she said admiring her handiwork after she was finished.

"Mmhmm," agreed Grandma, looking at herself in a hand mirror. "De ol' gyurl could still look pretty."

"Of course," agreed Jessica. "This is one sharp girl here." They both chuckled, and Jessica returned to the verandah, where she positioned herself to have a good view of the activities in the Bailey yard, without herself being noticed from down below.

Mr. Bailey had come home a few weeks before Christmas and repaired broken windows and doors, replaced old galvanize on the roof, and painted the entire house. It looked and smelled like new. All morning he was busy roasting a pig that had been slaughtered the day before. The yard had been cleared of all old tires and debris and Mr. Bailey had set up a big, colourful tent with extra chairs and tables underneath. There was a section for the live steel band that was expected.

"It look like big fête comin' up here?" Some nosy passers-by commented.

"I t'ink I gwine crash dis fête" others said.

Shark came out onto the verandah all dressed up in his pale gray suit and dark sun glasses. Since he lost his job this was the first time Jessica or anyone else was seeing him dressed in anything other than his shorts and sandals. Surprised, Jessica looked at him admiringly and said,

"Wo-o-oy! We must be going somewhere special!"

"Of course," he answered roughly. "I goin' to de weddin' nuh."

"You invited?" Jessica knew for a fact that Shark was not invited to the wedding which both Flo and Chester tried to keep as small as possible. Shark steupsed loudly.

"I don' need no invitation...I's family. Invitation is for strangers."

"Family?" she asked, confused.

"Of course...I's family" he answered, looking at her as if she'd just dropped from outer space. "You don' know dat me fader an' Ma Bailey is god cousins?" Jessica said nothing. She'd heard of god parents and even god sisters and brothers, but this god cousin bit was taking it a step too far.

The wedding reception went on well into the wee hours of the morning. Shark was not the only uninvited guest that showed up. Many residents from Rockville attended. A group of regulars at *Percy's* was quite conspicuous. Mr. and Mrs. Bailey welcomed one and all. Everyone toasted the bride and groom and danced and sang and ate and drank to their hearts' content. Madge came up the hill on more than one occasion with a plate for Jessica, who despite her sore back, got up many times to 'shake it up' on the verandah to the sounds of the steel band music from down below.

"Guess who just finish makin' big speech down there," Madge said at one time to Jessica, who almost dropped the plate when she heard it was Shark.

"He got more guts than boli," Jessica said.
Madge laughed.

"He talk a whole set of crap about family and closeness. He even call you his dearly beloved sister." Jessica's mouth was hanging open. "Daddy finally had to nudge him to stop, otherwise he would a' never stop spoutin'."

"Good for your Daddy."

"And I never know Ma Hilly could dance so...girl!" exclaimed Madge. "You should see those fancy moves she givin' them down there."

"Yes" smiled Jessica. "Dancing in her bones."

"You know Jess...if we look half as good as your grandmother when we reach her age, we'll be doin' great." Jessica nodded her agreement.

****

Early one Friday morning in February, Jessica gave birth to twins - a beautiful, healthy boy and girl. No one was more surprised than Jessica herself by the double birth. Grandma was by her side throughout, holding her hand, wiping her face and helping the district nurse. Aunt Mattie fetched and boiled water and did whatever the nurse asked. After he went to phone the doctor, Shark stayed on the verandah - he couldn't stomach the sounds coming from the next room. By the time Dr. Miller arrived, the twins were already born and their mother was resting comfortably.

Two days after the birth, Jessica got another big surprise. Her father came up the hill to visit her. She hadn't seen him since she'd left Willow Lane. She wasn't sure if she was imagining it, but he looked thin and tired. Ian was surprised to see Jessica looking so maternal and pretty in a beautiful lacy, pink, bed jacket. He approached her sitting up in the bed and embraced her warmly. He stroked the tiny cheeks and put his finger into the little hands of each tiny baby squinting up at him, as they lay on a makeshift cradle in the corner of the room; his grandchildren.

"I been meanin' to come see you since before Christmas," he said apologetically, "but you know how it is."

"How did you hear of the birth?" Jessica was curious to find out. She did not send any message to her father, whom she felt was keeping so distant for months now.

"You know how it is...somebody come in the store and mention it."

"My...news can travel fast," Jessica smiled. "How my darling little Trevor and Debbie doing?" Jessica did not inquire about Albertine.

"They doing okay," her father replied. "Trevor always asking for you and Debbie too."

"I miss them so much," she said softly, but in a louder tone asked "And how is the store?" She knew things must be hectic with Fleurina no longer there. Flo had resigned and she and Chester left for England a month after their wedding. Ian shrugged his shoulders.

"It goin'" he answered. "We have a new girl in the sewing section now, but it gwine take her a while to come up to speed. You know how it is." Was that sadness or worry Jessica was glimpsing in the corner of her father's eyes? She wasn't sure.

"I brought a crib for the babies and a few little things from the store," Ian continued.

"You brought a crib?" Jessica was both surprised and excited.

"Thanks a lot Dad," and she hugged him. A small smile escaped from his lips.

Grandma entered the room with a tray of soft drinks and sponge cake, made specially for visitors, during this time.

"Mr. Farrow...thanks for all de groceries and stuff you bring," she said to Ian. Turning to Jessica she said, "yoh father bring up a whole lot of stuff" and as she began to enumerate the items, Jessica's eyes grew wider and wider with amazement.

"I thought you said you brought a few little things," Jessica said, quoting her Dad, after hugging and thanking him again. She realized that despite opposition from his wife, her father was making a huge effort to bridge the gap between them and she appreciated it. It was then she made the decision to include 'Ian' in her son's name.

She called her son Joshua Martin Ian. Martin was the name of Pappy - her maternal grandfather whom she never knew. Her daughter, she named Jolene Hilda Audrey. Grandma moved her meager belongings once again. This time she curtained off a section of the living room which she used for her own bedroom, leaving the big room for Jessica and the babies. The crib that Ian brought was placed in the corner of the room.

CHAPTER 10

For forty days, Jessica did little else but rest and take care of the babies. This was Grandma's rule and she insisted on it, even though after a week or two, Jessica felt she was back to normal. Aunt Mattie enjoyed rocking the babies to sleep on the verandah. Grandma cautioned her to clean up herself, if she wanted to rock the twins and stressed that there must be no pipe smoking or drinking. Jessica noticed that after finishing up her chores, Aunt Mattie always showered in the back yard and changed into something clean. She hadn't seen her with her pipe for a while now and the putrid smell of stale alcohol had disappeared from her breath.

Shark surprised her. He seemed to delight in playing with the twins. Sometimes both himself and his mother could be seen on the verandah playing with or rocking the babies. Madge or one of the other Baileys would often come and take the twins for a walk in the garden or down the hill to the Bailey's home. Lenox made them a carriage with wheels big enough to accommodate the rough terrain of the hill. Jessica insisted on safety straps and a lot of padding for comfort.

With all this love and attention the babies flourished. Their different personalities gradually became apparent. Joshua slept and ate more. Jolene cried more and laughed more. They both mastered the art of walking, long before their first birthday.

Jessica was anxious to resume teaching to contribute to the household which now had two more little ones to support. She contacted all her students and tried to set up a schedule to continue classes. That's when she discovered that the parish priest had been undermining her. Father was telling the parents of her students that Jessica was an unfit mother - not being married - and therefore an unfit teacher as well. Jessica was furious. Had she not just baptized the twins, she would have chosen another church. It was bad enough she had to wait an extra week for their Baptism, as her children were 'unlawful' and could not be baptized on the Sunday for 'lawful' children.

"I'm so vexed" she said to Madge, as she sat on her bed, propped up with cushions, breast feeding Joshua. Jolene was still fast asleep. "I feel like going down there and giving that priest a piece of my mind." But Madge was the voice of reason.

"You know how everybody already think the priest can do no wrong…"

"Yeh…he like a little God."

"If you go down there and curse him off, he'll just use that against you."

Jessica agreed Madge had a point.

"But what I'm going to do? I must get something soon." Jessica knew that it wouldn't be long before Grandma's bank account would be completely depleted. Tutoring was the ideal position for her right now, because of the babies. Before her confinement, she had no less than twelve students and was doing very well.

"As soon as exams finish in June" said Madge, "I'm going to apply to go to Canada on the domestic scheme."

Jessica had heard a bit about this, but not in depth.

"Why you don't apply too?" she suggested to Jessica.

"But now I have children, how I could go?" The last thing on Jessica's mind right now was leaving her children to go abroad. It was already becoming clear to her that she would have to seek employment with one of the firms in town or with the civil service. Just the thought of leaving the children during the day weighed heavily on her mind.

Madge went towards the crib to get Jolene, who was beginning to wake up. "Hi Doux Doux" she cooed to the baby. "Let your godmother change you, before yoh mammie have to feed you." She got a clean diaper from the shelf and changed the baby as Jessica finished feeding Joshua. They exchanged babies.

"They give you a form to fill out, and my friend Nora say…if you have any children, just don't put that down on the form," said Madge, still referring to the domestic scheme in Canada.

"Whaat?" Were they expecting her to deny her children, just to go up to Canada to work as a domestic? Somebody must be mad somewhere.

Madge continued "They want single women, with no children."

"Me, I ain't leaving my children to go no place" Jessica said in a determined tone.

****

Jessica got employment at the medical health center in town. At first she missed the babies a lot. She fought hard to keep back the tears, that first morning as she boarded the bus for St. George's. Gradually she grew to accept her new position. At least she was bringing in a steady salary to the household. To give Shark his due, he helped a lot in the care of the twins. Grandma assured her that she was not to worry, everything would be fine. Eventually she began to cease worrying but she felt deprived. She missed all the babies' first events - the first steps, the first words - she was not the one who noticed even the first teeth, which came out in each mouth simultaneously.

    Now that she worked in town, she saw her father more frequently. He mentioned that business in the sewing section of *Best Bargains* had declined considerably. Albertine no longer went down to the hotels, as they couldn't meet the deadlines. The young lady that replaced Fleurina was no longer with them. Jessica was getting used to the worry lines around Ian's eyes.

    "We have to get another line," he admitted to her. At Jessica's request, he brought Trevor and Debbie to see her one lunch time at the conference room in the health center. She ate her bagged lunch there every day. She couldn't believe how much the children had grown in the space of a year. There were subtle changes in their personalities too. Trevor, who used to be so expressive, was now a little shy with her. Debbie didn't smile at all. She refused the carrot muffins that Jessica brought from home specially for them.

    "The Baileys having their annual beach picnic on Sunday," Jessica said to Ian. "Why don't you come down and bring the children along?" She noticed Trevor's face light up between bites from his muffin.

"Where?…Grand Anse?" Ian asked.

"Mmhmm."

"You bringing the twins?"

"Of course."

"Okay…deal," Ian replied.

"I'm looking forward to seeing all those fancy strokes that you so good at" Jessica said to Trevor, who couldn't help smiling as she ruffled his hair playfully. Debbie remained serious. "And Debbie, I can make your favorite sweet bread, if you like." Coconut sweet bread used to be a big hit with Debbie.

"No thanks," Debbie replied unconvincingly.

"I'll bring it anyway…for whoever wants."

It rained incessantly during the night and early that morning. Jessica was the first to rise. She went into the tiny kitchen to prepare the babies' bottles for the day. Looking out at the back yard through the kitchen window, she saw little rivulets spiraling down the hill. The wind during the night had undone some of the galvanize roof of the out house and the door of the shower stall that Mr. Bailey had installed for Grandma, was loose again. The home, which at one time housed just herself and Grandma comfortably, now had more than doubled its occupancy and was bursting at the seams.

She dreamed of adding on an extension, with another bedroom, flush toilet and a decent bathroom. The smell from the outhouse was a big embarrassment. But before that they needed to install electricity. Or was it more important to get a new railing and gate put on the verandah? That was a big safety concern for her - especially when the twins begin walking.

Jessica's head was in a twirl as she heard Grandma get up and tinkle into the pot, she kept underneath her bed.

"Dey gwine have to cancel de beach picnic" Grandma said, coming into the kitchen.

"Let's give it time" Jessica said, trying to be optimistic. This was the first opportunity that Trevor and Debbie were getting to see Joshua and Jolene and she hoped it wouldn't fall through. She heard Aunt Mattie stirring in the back room. Aunt Mattie's first job every morning was to empty and wash all the chamber pots. Since she had to pass through the kitchen with them, Jessica was waiting for her to finish this task before she herself began cooking some pelau for the picnic.

In the corner of the kitchen was an icebox with milk. There was still some ice there, so the milk should keep for the rest of the day. *A refrigerator would be nice.* She took two bottles from the icebox to feed the babies when they woke up. She placed them on the dining room table. While waiting for Aunt Mattie to finish her business, she went to check on the babies. Jolene was awake and playing happily with Joshua's nose and ears, while he slept. She tickled the chest of her chubby little daughter, who smiled back at her. She lifted her out of the crib.

"Hi girlieken...let Mummy change oo." Jessica never ceased being amazed by her babies. There had never been any baby anywhere more beautiful than her two. She never thought that her heart could reach such profound depths. She loved them so dearly. There was nothing better than spending time with them and watching them grow and discover the world. Every day they made a new discovery. Because she didn't want to ever forget this period, one of the first things Jessica purchased, when she started working, was a camera. She showed Grandma how to use it, but most of the time when she wasn't at home, it was Shark who took pictures of the babies.

By midmorning the sun shone brilliantly. The picnic was definitely on. The bus, *Sensational,* was almost packed to capacity by the time it left the Bailey home in Rockville. Yet there was another stop in Richmond. When Jessica saw the number of people waiting for the bus in Richmond, she was sure that some would have to be left behind. Not so. Everyone got on board. Both babies sat on Jessica's lap, while Madge sat on Grandma. Shark, with his dark glasses, was busily directing the sardine-like packing of the bus. They arrived safely at Grand Anse beach, with Lenox skillfully maneuvering the bus along the curvy, narrow roads, while leading everyone in the popular song

Enjoy yourself…it's later than you think.

Debbie and Trevor were already on the beach with their Dad, waiting patiently for Jessica's arrival with the twins. Both children were fascinated with the babies.

"I'm your auntie" Debbie said to Jolene, lifting her up, to kiss her soft cheek. "You have to call me Auntie Debbie." Jessica and Ian exchanged secret smiles. Debbie was so proud to be an 'auntie'.

Trevor finally got to show off what a fish he was. Everyone complimented him. Much to Jessica's horror though, he was determined to teach the babies to swim. She relaxed a bit when she saw several adults, including her father, around Trevor and baby Josh. As usual, the water at Grand Anse beach was as calm as it was clear.

Joshua seemed at home in the water and actually blew bubbles and gurgled. After a while Trevor exchanged Josh with Jolene, who laughed and splashed in the water as if that was her natural environment.

"We have two flying fish here," Ian pointed out to Jessica.

Grandma and Mrs. Bailey spent most of the time lying on the shore and catching up on the latest bits of gossip. Mrs. Bailey kept an anxious eye out for Jacob, especially when he was in the water. At times Madge, Jessica and several others from Rockville and Richmond joined the two ladies relaxing on the shore.

"How Flo and Chester doin'?" one lady asked Mrs. Bailey.

"Not bad…but dey say life not so easy in England."

Actually, Fleurina had written home saying that England was a big disappointment. As soon as she and Chester were finished with their studies, they were getting out of there. She discouraged Madge from following in her footsteps, which was the original plan.

Jessica took as many pictures as she could that day. She got Grandma and Mrs. Bailey lying on the sand with Jolene and Josh. She got another one with her Dad, Trevor, Debbie and the twins in the water. There was one shot of the meal set up on the picnic tables, with everyone standing around. She took a picture of Shark making a sand castle with the twins and Shark took one of Jessica, Madge and the twins. She got Jacob showing off his collection of sea shells to his mother and others.

They all had an enjoyable day. Debbie and Trevor ate like there was no tomorrow. Debbie 'polished off' all of the coconut sweet bread. Jessica promised them that she would bring the twins over to Willow Lane sometime. She was careful not to specify a time, as it would have to be when the queen was away. Since the bus was so crowded, Ian offered to drive them home.

"Thanks Mr. Farrow," Grandma said loudly, before Jessica could politely refuse. "Dat's a good idea." Then turning around, she called to Mrs. Bailey. "Hey Ethel...come wid us...we goin' wid Mr. Farrow." Jessica saw some of the people on the bus sigh with relief as Mrs. Bailey easily took up two seats. So with Grandma in the front seat, beside Ian, and Mrs. Bailey occupying most of the back seat, Jessica, the twins, Trevor and Debbie had to be crammed into the remaining space.

"I can't breathe here," Debbie complained, prompting Ian to ask Grandma and Mrs. Bailey to exchange seats. It made a huge difference. Ian dropped off the children at Willow Lane first, then continued on to Rockville. After Mrs. Bailey and Grandma left the car, Ian helped Jessica up the hill with the babies.

"Thanks so much, Daddy."

"I think everyone enjoy themselves today." He handed the baby he was carrying to Jessica, as he approached the verandah and kissed all three goodbye. "And by the way...I'm going away next week...okay?"

"You going away? Where to?" Jessica stopped immediately. It was the first time she was hearing of this trip.

"I'm going to Trinidad next week."

"Holiday?" Jessica was confused.

"No...I'm going for treatment at the St. E. hospital there."

CHAPTER 11

Madge passed her O Level exams with flying colours. There was great rejoicing in the Bailey household. She was the first Bailey to go to high school and get this far academically.

"Come later this evening leh we have a drink on dat," her brother Lenox said to Jessica the day the results came out. She was on her way home from work on board his bus, when Lenox flashed her a gold toothed smile, while effortlessly steering the bus around dangerous corners.

So that evening with a group of neighbours, Jessica and Grandma dropped by to say 'Cheers' to Madge. Mrs. Bailey baked an orange cake for the occasion. Lenox brought out a bottle of scotch, that his father kept hidden in the very back of his clothes closet, for special occasions. He had just taken out the scotch, when Mrs. Bailey spotted Shark and a couple of his friends from *Percy's* coming into the yard.

"Hurry" she said. "Get de empty bottle." Quickly she poured a little bit of the whisky from the original bottle of scotch into a second identical bottle, kept for this purpose. There were some known 'boozers' in the community, that seemed to appear out of nowhere whenever free booze was being served. They also had the reputation of remaining until the last drop. This way they would be tricked into thinking that there was not much to start with.

Lenox and his mother served the little gathering with drinks and cake. Jessica opted for rum punch instead of scotch on the rocks. Some had soft drinks. Everyone toasted Madge's success and sang

For she's a jolly good person…hip..hip..hooray!

"So…somebody here pass exams?" asked Shark, holding his glass to his friend for another drink from the bottle of scotch, which was now almost empty. It was obvious to all that Shark and the others from *Percy's* didn't have a clue what the celebration was all about.

"Yeeeh" stammered Jacob, as the youngest brother, Julian continued "Madge pass the O Levels." Lenox was happy that his mother had spotted them in the nick of time.

"Oh good" Shark answered, showing little to no enthusiasm, his eyes on the bottle instead.

After everyone left, Madge accompanied Jessica up the hill and they both sat on her bed to chat for a while. The children were fast asleep.

"I'm going tomorrow to apply to go to Canada on the domestic worker scheme," Madge informed Jessica.

"But you not a domestic…you just pass O Levels for heaven sake." There was a hint of annoyance in Jessica's voice.

"It's a way to get in to Canada…I don't intend to do that forever."

"Is that the only way to get in?"

"Well when you hear of another way...let me know," Madge replied curtly, sensing but not appreciating Jessica's opposition.

"When the next batch of girls leaving?"

"Not till next year April...but I have to get passport and medical...and a whole lot of stuff before." Jessica breathed a sigh of relief. At least it wasn't right away. At this moment she just couldn't stand the thought of Madge, her best friend, leaving Grenada and leaving her.

"When you going to know if they choose you?"

"The selection taking place next month...we should know soon after that."

Jessica decided to change the subject. Frankly it was getting her down. She wanted her friend to pursue her dreams, but in the bottom of her stomach she felt a twinge of envy.

"Any news from Flo?" Fleurina wrote to her mother every single week, since she left home.

"Oh yes," Madge's eyes lit up. She obviously had some breaking news.

"You know at the hospital where she training, she ran into Louisa..."

"Louisa?"

"Yes...and she pregnant, girl. It seems she and Jack got married some time ago." Jessica exhaled. She wasn't sure if she wanted to hear anything about Jack.

"Flo said she looking really beat up...not like the same Louisa at all," Madge continued eagerly.

"Why, what's wrong?" *As if I really care.*

"She said Jack still not working...and it really hard for her. She said he having trouble getting the type of job he looking for."

Jessica saw it clearly. "I guess Mr. DeCoutreau has to get a high class, high paying job right away. No blue collar work for him...no siree!" she was very sarcastic. Madge grimaced.

"You know...I think you have a point...that may be part of Jack's problem." Then standing up to leave, she said to Jessica as she held the bedroom door open. "I don't care if I have to stoop to conquer...if I have to do domestic work to get where I want, then so be it." The door quietly shut behind her. *Sometimes Madge Bailey can make a damn lot of sense!*

****

Jessica went to Willow Lane to visit her father, as soon as she heard he had returned from Trinidad. Ian had prostate cancer and was undergoing chemotherapy. The word 'cancer' was like the tolling of the death bell to him. It took a lot of detective work on Jessica's part, before she uncovered his true diagnosis. He was sitting in the living room when she arrived. His skin was sallow and he had lost all his hair. The house was in need of a good cleaning. The living room which Jessica used to keep immaculate, was in dire need of dusting and sweeping. There were round glass stains on the center table and someone's shoes were left at the door.

"You look like Yul Bryner, Dad." Jessica tried a crude attempt at humour, stroking her father's bald head. Ian smiled weakly.

"How you feeling, Dad?" she became serious.

"Not bad today."

"So some days you feel good and some days bad?"

"Some days bad and some days worse," he replied.
Jessica had to pull out of him, what the doctor said about his prognosis. He didn't know. Was the treatment having any effect on the tumor? The doctor didn't say. Had he finished with the chemotherapy? Yes…well sort of. When was he going back to see the doctor?

"You know how it is…everything cost so much money…nothing was planned." Jessica couldn't believe her ears. Certainly her father and Albertine had enough money to deal with his illness? But she wasn't sure. Yes, they lived in Willow Lane. Yes, they had a business which recently was going down hill steadily, she reminded herself. She realized that faced with some illnesses, one's life savings could go poof just like air. She realized why recently there was always a worried look in her father's eyes. Just thinking about it, made Jessica feel sick.

The children came home during Jessica's visit. They were delighted to see her, but disappointed that she hadn't brought the twins.

"Next time," she promised. "This visit is for Daddy."

****

Aunt Mattie's moods seemed to keep pace with the rocking chair - forward and backward, backward and forward. Whenever there was a sighting of Jacob under the cocoa, she would get upset and her mood would swing backward. Grandma already told her that it was okay for Jacob to help himself to the mangoes. After all, he was a Bailey and she couldn't count the number of times one of them had done some good deed for her. They were like family. Cyprian had repaired the outhouse and the shower stall. Whenever Lenox went hunting, he brought her back manicou or tattoo - something to put in her pot. So at the very least they could have some mangoes.

But Aunt Mattie was adamant. "You never t'ief dey stuff - dey give dem to you" she said, as soon as Grandma was out of hearing range. Seeing Jessica nearby, and knowing she had an audience, she continued.

"Dat woman done t'ief enough from me already."

"Who? Ma Bailey?" Jessica asked puzzled.

"She self." Back and forth went the rocking chair, as Aunt Mattie puffed on her pipe. Jessica was keeping one eye on the children playing in the front yard.

"What it is Ma Bailey t'ief from you Auntie?" Aunt Mattie blew out a puff of smoke before she answered quietly,

"Dat same Dawson nuh."

"She t'ief your husband?" Jessica asked in surprise. "But why?...she got her own husband."

"Listen to me...half dem children she have dey, is Dawson own." The plot was certainly thickening. Is that why Aunt Mattie never befriended the Baileys - particularly Mrs. Bailey?

"Now Auntie...it's not nice to say stuff like that about people."

"It not nice for she do what she do neider," retorted Aunt Mattie, drawing on her pipe.

"And how you know half her children is for Uncle Dawson?" Jessica was getting to the bottom of this.

"Well maybe not half...but for sure de two oldest."

Jessica stared at Aunt Mattie in disbelief. *That would be Terri and Lisa.* Aunt Mattie continued. "Cyprian spen' most of de time in dose days pickin' apple in America. Dat was when she trick Dawson into foolin' wid her." This story was getting wilder by the minute. As if reading her mind, Aunt Mattie stood up, pulled a little aluminum container from some deep pocket of her petticoat, opened it, and took out a note browned with age that had been folded over many times.

"Look…I have de letter she write Dawson. Look…read it nuh."

Loud screams sounded from down below, interrupting Jessica as she was about to take the note from Aunt Mattie. She rushed down the steps to pick up Jolene, who had wandered down the slope of the hill and fallen face down in the dirt.

"Oh…poor little Joly," Jessica comforted her daughter picking her up. She also got hold of Joshua at the same time. Grandma came to the verandah to see what the screaming was about.

"I'm going to give them a bath now," Jessica said, going in from the verandah through the kitchen door. Both children were filthy from playing in the yard. The note and the aluminum container had disappeared from sight. Aunt Mattie rocked to and fro in the rocking chair.

****

That April, Madge was one of six young ladies from Grenada to leave for Canada on the domestic workers' scheme. Jessica went to the airport with the Baileys to see her off. She couldn't stop the tears.

"Don't cry Jessie," Madge said, her own tears not far away. "We'll always be best friends."
On the drive back to Rockville, Ma Bailey who had been strong all along, broke down and wept.

"Well…me last gyurl chile gone now," she sobbed.

"She not gone Mammie," Julian comforted his mother, putting one arm around some of her. "She just gone from home…and besides she just hours away by plane." *Was this little Julian being so mature? Gosh time sure flies.*

CHAPTER 12

Jessica and the twins were lying on the floor of the verandah, colouring pictures of animals in a colouring book. The blossoms of the flamboyant tree bobbed up and down, some yielding to the intensity of the breeze.

"Now what did this chicken say to the pussy cat?" she asked Joshua, pointing to the page he had just coloured. Josh thought for a while - he was always the more pensive of the two, when Jolene butted in quickly,

"Chicken say 'putty cat…putty cat…go away!'"
The chicken certainly was looking at the cat menacingly.

"That's right" Jessica responded. Jolene clapped her hands joyfully, happy that she had the right answer. Joshua clapped too then added

"Or else I beat you up…bust up yoh mout."
Now where was he learning this beat you up, burst up your mouth thing? Jessica hugged both children. They were now three and a half years old and growing happily and healthily. She had so much to be thankful for.

Grandma joined them on the verandah, sitting on the rocking chair. Josh got up from where he was lying to go sit in Grandma's lap. That was his favorite place to be. Jessica remembered when that used to be her favorite spot too. He loved the smell of fresh herbs that Grandma always seemed to exude.

"You don't want to colour this rabbit, Josh?" Jessica encouraged him, but Josh had already entwined his arms tightly around Grandma's neck. It was almost nap time and he soon fell fast asleep. Lying against her mother on the floor, her fingers red from the crayons, Jolene was not far from sleep either.

"We going to get some good rain tonight," Grandma said, feeling the breeze and looking in the direction of the mountains. That reminded Jessica of something she wanted to discuss with Grandma. It was always a mess in the back yard when it rained, and that outhouse simply had to go.

"Grandma, for Christmas this year…would be nice if we can add on a bathroom with flush toilet and proper shower to the back by the kitchen." She knew this was a big project which would more than deplete their bank account, but she badly wanted to have that done. She didn't want the children growing up knowing anything about an outhouse. That was the dark ages.

"Darlin' everyt'ing take money…but first t'ings must come first."

"But that's important Ma…"

"We already make a lot of big changes 'round here. We have water in de kitchen now and we even have electricity." Grandma spoke as if they were living in the lap of luxury. Jessica wanted to buy a fridge as well. She was tired of that safe and icebox, but Grandma vetoed it. It wasn't necessary she said. There were a lot more important things than that, she felt. Consequently Grandma was not given the chance to reject the twin bunk beds of white lacquered steel that Jessica recently purchased for the children, who had long ago outgrown their crib.

Grandma changed Joshua's position in her lap. After he settled back down, she turned to Jessica.

"You know Jessie…is time you make a move. Don't waste dose brains dat God give you, chile." Jessica felt her heart jump. She knew exactly what her grandmother was going to say. She had been thinking the same thing recently, but she just couldn't bear having to leave her children behind. Grandma continued.

"I'm gettin' on Jessie…although God still give me health an' strength. But it not gwine last forever." Grandma stroked Joshua's back. Jessica pulled Jolene's dress down over her bum.

"Instead of usin' de money on bathroom, why you don' try go to Canada an' see how you can make a better life for you an' de children?" Yes…this is what she was expecting. Jessica looked down at her sleeping daughter and then across at Joshua fast asleep in Grandma's lap. She didn't reply right away. Both herself and Grandma were visiting the Baileys when they received the fabulous news that Madge had obtained employment at the Royal Bank of Canada in Montreal. She had worked as a domestic for less than a year. Until recently, 'bank jobs' were generally reserved for the 'top' class in Grenada. Surely if Madge could swing that, it should be a piece of cake for Jessica.

"What about the children, Ma?"

"Don' worry bout de children. I t'ink I got a few more good years in me to take care o' dem. But you cyan' wait too long." It was bittersweet. Jessica felt a lump in her throat. This woman, who had raised her daughter, then granddaughter, was now offering herself one more time in the raising of her great grand children. But she was saying 'don't wait too long'. Jessica had never for one minute contemplated a world without Grandma.

****

Ian's cancer seemed to be in remission. Jessica begged God for this mercy, which He must have granted because three years later Ian was still cancer free. Although business was not booming at *Best Bargains*, they did not go under. Albertine started a new line of baby clothes and products, with which she was having some success. They seemed to be weathering the storm.

Jessica brought the twins down to Willow Lane one Saturday afternoon. It was a short visit but she had promised Trevor and Debbie to bring them. She arranged with her Dad to pick them all up at Willow Lane and take them to the fair at *St. Anne's* school. That was the big event in the town that day. The twins looked adorable in their matching sailor outfits and Debbie and Trevor were proud to act as their chaperons.

While the children played 'pinning the tail on the donkey', Jessica confided in her father her decision to follow Grandma's advice and go to Canada.

"That's good," Ian replied. "Life's getting too hard here and the political situation is not helping." He was referring to upheavals between the Gairy government that was now back in power and its opponents. Championing the cause of the working class against a repressive colonial rule, Gairy first came into power in 1951. Unfortunately, Ian and many other people came to feel, that Gairy simply wanted to replace a corrupt colonial system with one that was totally under his control. "If I was still young…I'd be gone from here in a jiffy."

"You think things going to get worse here?"

"Definitely. Your grandmother right girl…you go and make a life for yourself and the children."

****

Jessica ripped open the envelope. She always relished getting a letter from Madge. It was a long letter this time - three pages. Sometimes Madge included a page for Jessica, in one of her mother's letters. Sometimes there was a message for Jessica in a letter to one of the Baileys. Today she got her own long letter and as she unfolded it, two little photographs fell out. One was of Madge in her winter coat, hat, boots and gloves tossing some snow into the air. Only her face was exposed. The other was Madge standing beside a tall, slim, young man, similarly dressed. At the back of the picture was scribbled "Madge and Willie". Even though they were both smiling, they looked cold. Jessica lay across her bed and began reading the letter.

Jessica girl, you wouldn't believe this but Willie and I are planning to get married next year. Willie Johnson was a fellow from Guyana that Madge met while attending evening classes at Sir George William's University in Montreal. She had been writing about him for some time now, so actually the upcoming marriage did not surprise anyone. *I'm so glad to hear you applied to come up on the domestic scheme.* Jessica recalled the times when she was not enthusiastic about Madge being a domestic. Now she was going that same route herself. *I can't wait for you to come. Perhaps you can be my maid of honour at the wedding.*

Madge had her up in Canada already. The selection process hadn't even taken place yet. *Kiss my dear little godchildren for me and don't forget to send me some updated pictures of them.* Madge was a kind and loving godparent to the children. She never failed to inquire how they were doing. Sometimes she sent little gifts for them.

It was good hearing from Madge. She seemed so happy. She had a good job and had found true love. She wrote a lot about the cold weather. It was worse than she had anticipated, but she said once you got inside a building you didn't have to worry, as they were all centrally heated. Not like Fleurina, who was still in England. Flo complained of having to put coins in a meter to keep warm indoors. When the landlady discovered she was having a bath every day, she was told she was wasting the hot water. A weekly bath was all that was permitted.

"So you hear from Madge?" Ma Bailey was smiling from cheek to cheek. While she loved all her children dearly, it was obvious Madge was her shining star. It was always "Madge dis" or "Madge dat".

"So congrats…you having another wedding in the family?" Jessica said to Mrs. Bailey.

"Yes gyurl…and who knows…Flo may be able to make it."

"Flo?"

"But don' say nuttin'…dat gwine be a surprise for Madge." Flo had just completed her nursing course in London. There were big complications regarding her name, which she finally changed officially. Her mother had to get her an affidavit from the registry in Grenada to confirm that Fleurina Anastasia and Jane Elizabeth on her passport, were one and the same person. Chester had one more year to complete his engineering degree, but they agreed that since opportunities were opening up for nurses in Canada, Flo should go ahead to Canada and Chester would follow later.

****

The day was dark and gloomy. A hurricane was expected. Everyone who remembered 'Hurricane Janet' which blasted Grenada in 1955, was nervous. There was a collective sigh of relief when the hurricane was downgraded to a tropical storm. That same day the selection committee announced their choice of ladies for the domestic scheme in Canada. Jessica was not chosen. When the names were announced, hers was not among them. Even though she had tried not to count her chickens before they were hatched, she couldn't help feeling deeply disappointed.

"It all in God's hands Darlin'," Grandma remarked. She could sense the gloom overtaking Jessica. "Maybe you suppose to see de children through dey first day at school."

As usual, Grandma had a point. Jessica was struggling with mixed emotions. It would mean a lot to her to carry Josh and Jolene to kindergarten on their first day. It was unbelievable how fast they were growing. She still couldn't bear the thought of leaving them behind, to go to Canada, but she was determined to do whatever was needed, to give them the best life she could.

CHAPTER 13

In April of the following year, Jessica left Grenada for Montreal, Canada. Grandma, along with the twins, Ma Bailey, Lenox, Jacob and Julian, her Dad, Trevor and Debbie all came to the airport to see her off. She was replacing one of the originally selected ladies, who had opted to return to Grenada, having discovered that Canada was just not her 'cup of tea'. So in a way, Jessica was able to 'have her cake and eat it too'. She was able to see her children off for their first day at kindergarten.

Jessica was told she was going to work for a Mr. and Mrs. Bernstein in Montreal. Arrangements had been made that they would meet her at the airport on her arrival, and take her to their home. That whole week, friends dropped by to wish Jessica good bye and good luck.

She made some private time to talk with Aunt Mattie and encouraged her to let go of the past. She never did get to read that letter in the little aluminum container.

"I know how it hurts, Auntie…but let it go…we can't let what other people do eat away at our insides. It's not good to give them that power." In giving this advice she drew from her own experiences as well. Over the years, the hurt that Jack had inflicted on her heart, had completely healed. She seldom thought of him and did not bear him any ill will. She put her arms around her withered aunt.

"Promise me you going to try Auntie." Aunt Mattie returned the embrace, as she nodded.

"God keep you safe Darlin'," she said. "An' never mind yoh ol' auntie...she gwine come through."

"That's the stuff I want to hear," said Jessica encouragingly. She kissed her aunt's cheek, and tasted something wet and salty.

Shark was very seldom at home. If he came in at all, it was in the wee hours of the morning when Jessica was asleep. According to Aunt Mattie, he got a new job recently. He was hired by one of the hotels to take tourists around the island on sightseeing tours but rumour had it that he was working as a male prostitute at the hotel. Jessica left him a little note telling him good bye and wishing him the very best.

The flight was scheduled for twelve thirty. That morning Jessica rolled the wash tub into the kitchen and filled it with warm water. As she bathed the children in the tub, she couldn't help thinking 'This is the last time, I'm going to get to do this.' She soaped them and rinsed them off with extra special care. They had both gotten so dark now, that the blue birth marks on their bums could not be seen any more. She brought them into the bedroom, draped in towels, dressed them and combed their hair.

"Tickle...tickle...tickle" said Jolene, wanting to be playful. She didn't understand why their mother was so quiet this morning. Jessica had hardly eaten breakfast and she had a dull headache. She was trying her very best not to cry.

The twelve thirty flight didn't eventually leave till three thirty. Luckily Grandma had packed some fried chicken and bread. She noticed that Jessica had not eaten anything that morning. They bought some soft drinks at the airport. When the announcement finally sounded for passengers to get in line, with their boarding passes, it was time to say good bye.

Jessica hugged and kissed everyone. She tightly embraced her father, Trevor and Debbie, then turned to Grandma. They held each other tightly as the tears flowed freely down their cheeks.

"God bless you chile…God be with you always, my Darlin'," said Grandma.

"I'm goin' to miss you so much, Grandma." Jessica turned to the children, who seeing their mother and Grandma crying, were now beginning to cry too. She could hardly speak. She wondered when she was going to see them again.

"Bye Darling…bye Sweetheart…Mummy loves you both so much."

"Bye Mummy."
She wrapped her arms around them both and sobbed uncontrollably.

There was another delay in Barbados and Jessica did not arrive in Montreal until eleven thirty that night. It was freezing cold when she stepped off the plane. The thick sweater she wore made no difference at all. She felt like she had been dunked in ice cold water. The few steps from the plane to the terminal seemed to take forever. *It's supposed to be spring now. If winter is colder than this, God help us.*

Because of all the delays, she was not surprised that Mr. and Mrs. Bernstein were not there to meet her. Luckily, thanks to Madge, she had a few Canadian coins. After she got her luggage from the carousel, she looked around for a phone booth and tried the number that she was given for the Bernstein's. No one answered. She tried again. This time she lost her quarter in the machine. She had one more quarter. She decided to call Madge, who had gotten married to Willie two weeks before. "Please God let them be home," Jessica prayed. Madge answered on the sixth ring. She sounded as though she'd been fast asleep. Jessica almost wept with joy.

"Madge...it's me. I'm at the airport."

"Jessie?"

"Yes girl...I'm at the airport and nobody's here to meet me."

"The Bernsteins didn't come for you?"

"Well...the flight was delayed...I tried calling them...but nobody's answering."

"Jessie...take a taxi and come over to our home." That made sense but Jessica didn't have a clue how she was going to do that. Besides it was freezing outside. It was like asking her to step into the mouth of a beast.

"Can you come get me?" Jessica was almost in tears. She felt lonely and abandoned.

"Yes...let me wake up Willie...but it'll take a good hour before we reach you." Madge was fully awake now and accurately summed up the situation.

"I'll sit and wait...I'm by the Air Canada counter."

"Okay...see you in a while, Jess."

Her head hurt, her throat hurt, she felt miserable and sick. She wasn't sure if this was the result of the emotional trauma she had undergone that day, or whether she was in fact coming down with some bug. But Jessica was relieved to make contact with her friend Madge, who was on her way to rescue her.

Madge and Willie arrived at the airport in a little less than an hour.

"Jessie!" she heard Madge, before she actually spotted her. They ran to each other and embraced. "Willie's gone to park the car. He'll be here shortly." It was great seeing Madge. She had put on some weight and looked more like her mother now. And she actually had a slight Canadian accent - the way she said 'shortlay'.

"Sorry…to wake y'all up like this," Jessica began to apologize.

"I tried calling the Bernsteins earlier, to find out if you got in safely, and no one answered then either," Madge said, then below her breath murmured "those bums!"

"Thanks for being there for me, Madge."

"I brought some of my winter gear to loan you… this coat, boots and tuque and scarf." Madge opened the sports bag she was carrying and took out the items, helping Jessica into them. The coat did not come down to Jessica's knees, but the boots were a good fit and the tuque and scarf made her feel warm and cozy.

Willie joined them then. He had the height of a basketball player, with kind, friendly eyes.

"Is this all your luggage?" he asked after Madge introduced her husband to her best friend. Jessica nodded. She was relieved to give up her hand luggage which now felt like a ton of lead.

They arrived at the little St. Marc's street apartment around two a.m. Jessica was exhausted. Montreal looked bleak and dismal. Madge pulled out the hide-a-bed in the living room. After a hot cup of green tea, Jessica snuggled down between a comforter and sheet that smelled sweetly of lavender and fell fast asleep.

****

She felt a whole lot better when she awoke later that morning. As she lay in bed earlier on, in between sleep and wake, she imagined herself as a little girl again with her mother rocking her gently.

"Everything's going to be okay," Audrey said, as she kissed Jessica then laughed loudly. The sound of this loud laughter completely awakened Jessica. She listened for a moment then realized it was Madge laughing loudly in the adjoining bedroom.

Madge and Willie had a small but very comfortable apartment. They sat at the little dining room table, separated by a counter from the neat little kitchen and breakfasted on blood pudding and flying fish, which Ma Bailey had given Jessica to carry up for Madge.

"This is delicious," said Willie. Madge felt a bit guilty.

"I told Mammie not to load you up with stuff for me," she apologized. Jessica had also brought her a bottle of rum, a bottle of hot pepper sauce and some fruit cake. They had a lot of catching up to do. Jessica had to give a detailed account of everyone back home, starting with the twins. Her eyes moistened when she spoke of her babies.

"I have to send for them fast, fast" she told Madge and Willie.

They showed Jessica their wedding pictures, featuring Flo who stood right beside the couple.

"Does Flo live far from here?" Jessica asked.

"Yes. She left for Toronto last week. She has a job with a hospital there."

"Too bad she left before I got here…it would have been nice to see Flo."

"She's still tall and skinny just like you," Madge laughed, as she got up to clear the dishes from the table. "I'm the one that's starting to put on weight." Willie swatted her behind playfully, obviously not having a problem with her roundness.

"Flo mentioned she used to see Jack's wife from time to time," Madge continued. "They have three children now and Jack's still on 'the dole'. I don't believe he worked one solitary day since he arrived in England." Madge looked at the expression on Jessica's face - happy that she was the one giving her this shocking news.

Willie was warm and friendly. He was doing a biology and chemistry major part-time at Sir George William's university. There was a problem with one of the professors, he said. He thought this professor was racist. He kept marking down the black students in his class consistently. The racism was blatant. The students complained over and over and got no redress. Finally they staged a 'sit in' in the computer center of the university. Instead of the administration dealing with the issues fairly, the police were sent to forcefully remove the students and a riot broke out. Jessica remembered hearing about this on Radio Guardian from Trinidad, but didn't know a lot of the details which Willie filled in for her. Willie was so disgusted with SGWU that he wanted to switch universities. He was thinking of going to Ottawa and continuing in one of the universities there.

Jessica was to start working at the Bernsteins the next day. Before bringing her to the Bernstein's residence, they attended mass at a nearby French church and then they took her to see some of the sights of Montreal. The down town area was very impressive as was the famed St. Joseph's oratory.

"This is your little home away from home now," Madge said as they left the apartment that evening. Willie handed her a key.

"You're welcome here anytime," he said, making Jessica feel fortunate to have the support of such close friends as she began her stay in Canada.

****

Mrs. Bernstein answered the doorbell.

"Hello…you must be Jessica," she said, extending her hand with a smile. Jessica took it and smiled. "Put it down here," she said to Willie, who was bringing Jessica's heavy suitcase up the stairs to the landing. Since he was not invited in any further, he bid a hasty goodbye to Jessica, who waved at Madge sitting in their *Corolla*.

"We were expecting you since yesterday afternoon," Mrs. Bernstein went on to say. The smile had disappeared from her face.

"The plane was delayed…I tried calling here when I arrived last night."

"Yes…yes…we were at a function last night." Mrs. Bernstein seemed to brush off all explanations. "Well, bring your suitcase down here," she gestured for Jessica to follow her with her heavy suitcase. *Would have been nice if Willie could have helped me with this.*

The house seemed huge. *Can't be only four people living in this mansion.* As they passed a set of glass doors, which seemed like the entrance to an office, Mrs. Bernstein called out,
"Marty...she's here." That was Mr. Bernstein. He unfolded his lanky form from a swivel chair of leather and slowly slithered into the hallway to greet Jessica.
"Hello," he smiled. He did not offer his hand.
"Good evening," replied Jessica, returning the smile and trying to be polite. Neither did he offer help with the suitcase, as she followed Mrs. Bernstein further down the hallway and down some stairs.
"This is your room," she said, opening a door and flicking on the lights. "You'll meet Bernard and April tomorrow. They're asleep now."
"Thank you," Jessica replied. The room was relatively sparse. It contained a single bed, dresser, chair and built-in closet. Wearily, she put her suitcase down.
"There's a bathroom over here." Mrs. Bernstein said, opening an adjoining door and flicking on the lights.
"What time do you expect me up tomorrow?" Jessica asked, as Mrs. Bernstein was about to leave.
"The children get up around eight," she said, not responding directly to Jessica's question, "and the school bus picks them up at nine." Then she was gone.

****

Jessica unpacked her suitcase, hanging her dresses in the closet and placing her nightgowns, underwear, hosiery, towels and toiletries into the drawers of the dresser. She left the little box with the golden J bracelet in her suitcase, which she put at the top shelf of the closet. On top of the dresser, she placed framed photographs of Josh and Jo with Grandma, her father with the twins, Trevor and Debbie that she had taken on the beach, the day of the Baileys' beach picnic and another one taken a long time ago with herself, Madge, Flo, Lenox, Jacob and Julian.

Before she went to bed that night, Jessica wrote a letter to her children, her grandmother and Aunt Mattie. *Just to let you know I arrived safely. Madge and Willie came to meet me at the airport.* No point telling them all the drama she went through. *I spent the day with Madge and Willie, who brought me over to the Bernsteins afterwards. Willie is a darling. They have a lovely apartment. My dear pumpkins don't forget how much your Mummy loves you.* Now that they weren't together, she felt the need to remind her children of that. *It won't be long before we're together again. Listen to Grandma and Aunt Mattie. Do what they tell you and don't forget to say your prayers every night.* She folded the letter and enclosed it in an envelope. She was going to try to mail it the next day. She turned off the light and tried to go to sleep. She checked her watch. It was long after midnight and she still could not fall asleep. She feared that she would sleep-in the following morning, if sleep didn't come soon. That certainly won't be a good start. I must buy an alarm clock soon, she decided.

CHAPTER 14

There was a loud bang. Jessica bolted upright in her bed. "What was that?" she wondered and glanced at her watch. It was seven o' clock. She heard a car slowly backing out of somewhere nearby.

Jessica got out of bed. She decided that since she was awake she would shower and get dressed to start the day. When she was done she retraced her footsteps from the night before, back up the stairs. She easily found the kitchen with adjoining dinette. Various appliances, some of them new to Jessica, adorned the kitchen counters. The aroma from a coffee maker with fresh coffee, reminded her how much she craved some caffeine. The morning *Gazette* lay sprawled open on the dinette table. Since no one was around, Jessica sat on a stool facing the kitchen counter to read the papers.

She turned around to the sound of a rustle coming from above. She saw four little eyes peeping at her from the curve of the staircase.

"Hi" said Jessica, with a smile. They kept on staring at her.

"Hi" Jessica repeated. Then added in a friendly tone "I'm Jessica…you want to tell me your names?" Even though she knew what the children's names were, she used this strategy as an 'ice breaker'. The little girl came down a few more steps. She was four years old and was wearing a beautiful pair of pink cotton pajamas. Jessica got up from the stool and went towards her, holding out her arms. She hesitated for a while and then allowed Jessica to give her a little hug, while her brother, who was six, remained where he was with a scowl on his freckled face.

"What's your name?" Jessica asked the little girl, when she had released her.

"April," she replied.

"That's a pretty name." April grinned. "And those are some pretty pajamas you're wearing." The grin got broader as April looked down at herself to verify that she was indeed wearing some pretty pajamas. Her brother dashed down the stairs past them, running into the parlor beyond. Obviously envious of the attention April was getting, and looking for some focus on himself, he threw himself on the floor and began somersaulting. He almost knocked down a table with some expensive looking crystal figurines on it. Luckily, Mrs. Bernstein, wearing a thick bath robe, made an appearance at this time.

"Bernie…get out of there…you know you're not allowed in that room" she shouted. To Jessica she said, "They have bagels and cream cheese with apple juice for breakfast every morning."

"Good morning," Jessica stammered a greeting, taken aback by the lack of greeting from the lady of the house. "Where are they kept?"

"Today I'll do it," she said. "And you can watch me. Bernie!" she shouted again at her son still rolling on the floor in the parlor. She helped herself to a cup of coffee from the coffee maker. Three Bernies later, Bernie had still not left the parlor. He did so only when his mother physically removed him from there.

That first day, Jessica learned what her duties were. Basically, she was to take care of the children. She was to tidy their rooms, give them breakfast and snacks, dress them and see them off to school in the school bus and meet them when the school bus brought them back. She had Thursdays and Sundays off. She was surprised that there was so little cooking taking place in that huge kitchen. She was only expected to give the children breakfast and snacks and fix meals for herself. Mr. and Mrs. Bernstein ate out more often than not. She found out that a cleaning woman came once a week to clean the mansion.

  She inquired where the post office was, where she could purchase some stamps and mail her letter. It was a few blocks east, but there was a mail box almost at the end of the driveway. After making sure that the children were safely on the school bus, Jessica went sightseeing on foot. Mrs. Bernstein had encouraged her to do so, giving her a key for the side entrance of the house. "Just make sure you're back to get the kids from the bus at three fifteen," she said.

  Traffic lights were new to Jessica. In St. George's, policemen with white gloves directed the traffic. She watched for a while and soon got the hang of it. She discovered the post office, a bank, pharmacy and grocery store were just minutes away. She entered the grocery store thinking she would purchase a few items. Everything seemed relatively cheap to what she was accustomed to in Grenada. Apples which cost a small fortune at home were dirt cheap here. *With all the fruit we have in Grenada, it's silly to be importing apples anyway.* Several buses passed by while she was out. The transportation system seemed to be great. She didn't know exactly how the system worked but was excited and eager to find out soon.

She turned around and retraced her footsteps home. She waved at Mrs. Bernstein, who was just leaving in her *Corvette*. She learned earlier that Mr. Bernstein managed a big corporation and left for work at seven every morning. The enormous garage was actually next to Jessica's bedroom, so that's why she heard clearly when he left that morning. After tidying the children's bedrooms and bathrooms - they each had their own - and making herself a light brunch, there was not much else for Jessica to do.

The phone rang.

"Hello," she answered. A male voice asked for Mrs. Bernstein.

"I'm sorry but Mrs. Bernstein is not at home now."

"Has she left already?"

"Yes...she's left. Whom should I say called?" But the person had already hung up. She put the receiver back and looked around her.

The house was huge. In the parlor, drapes swirled around in intricate patterns, from the ceiling to the floor occupying an entire wall. The fabric of the chairs matched the drapes. Huge oil paintings of wintry scenes adorned the walls. Across the hallway in the dining room, was an enormous dining table with seats, upholstered in rich velvet. A luxurious chandelier hung from the ceiling. Artificial trees, plants and flowers were everywhere.

Jessica felt somewhat chilly. She was about to go down to her bedroom to get her sweater when the phone rang again. It was Madge.

"Girl...what's happening?" It was heart warming to hear a familiar voice.

"Everything's going well," she answered. "The children are at school and Mrs. Bernstein is out."

"Enjoy your time when the children are out," Madge advised. "Most of these children here are spoilt little brats." Jessica smiled. She had already seen how Bernie acted with his mother that morning, but April was sweet.

"I went out for a little walk this morning. I posted a letter home."

"Already?...that's good. You off Thursdays?"

"Mmhmm," replied Jessica. "Thursdays and Sundays."

"I've got to go now," said Madge. "But on Thursday I'm taking the day off to take you shopping and show you around some more." Jessica smiled. She felt so grateful to have a friend like Madge. She needed to get some clothes for the winter, and she needed an alarm clock and she was going to buy some more writing equipment. She had decided to use her spare time writing poems and stories for her children at home.

At ten minutes after three, Jessica was waiting at the driveway for the return of the children by the school bus. Promptly at three fifteen the bus was at the driveway. Jessica was amazed and impressed by the precision.

"Hi," she said to the children as they alighted from the bus. April smiled and placed her little hand in Jessica's. Bernie scowled.

They all entered the home through the side entrance. The children took off their coats and threw them on the floor along with their school bags. They rushed to turn on the TV in the family parlor - a less formal room, closer to the kitchen. Jessica had already prepared their snacks, which she now placed on the dinette table.

"Go wash your hands," she instructed. "And then come have a snack."

"No," shouted Bernie as he rolled on the floor. "My hands are clean. Bring my snack here." *I'm going to have to be firm with this one.* She took April, who was split between obeying her and following Bernie, gently by the hand. She helped her change from her school clothes into what seemed like something more relaxed, washed and dried her hands, and together they went back downstairs. They could see Bernie, still lying on the floor in the TV room. Jessica got a glass of juice from the fridge for April and served her snack to her on a little glass plate. She ignored Bernie.

Realizing that no one was paying attention to him, Bernie slowly got up and shuffled into the dinette. He scowled at Jessica then tried to grab some of the goodies from the platter on the table.

"You're ready now?" Jessica asked looking directly at him and removing the platter from his reach. "You'll have to wash your hands first though...you don't want to eat with dirty hands...do you?"

He looked meanly at her then went to the kitchen sink and let a strong jet of water flow over his hands for a few seconds, making more of a mess on the counter for Jessica to clean up afterwards. Jessica was sure this was deliberate.

"There" he said, shaking his dripping hands at Jessica and April. "I washed my hands."

"Go dry them in the paper towel, please" Jessica asked pointing to the roll of paper towel hanging from the cupboard. He chose instead to dry them in his sweater. Jessica stared at him in displeasure but allowed him to have his snack. *If this were my six year old, I know what I'd do.* Jessica tidied up the kitchen and dinette after the children were done.

Mrs. Bernstein came in around six and by six thirty she and the children were eating supper. Jessica declined the offer of supper, opting to prepare her own meal herself. She was glad she did so. She saw Mrs. Bernstein put three big pieces of meat into a frying pan. *Just one of those would be more than enough for a Sunday dinner at Grandma's.* A few minutes on one side and a few minutes on the other, and each was ready to be served. That was it. Salt and pepper were sprinkled on afterwards. The fact that the blood ran out of the meat as they cut into it, seemed not to bother them in the least.

Jessica couldn't help noticing that Bernie's behavior was much worse when his mother was present. She was relieved when after supper, it was time for them to shower and go to bed.

"Would you like me to read you a bed time story?" she asked April. In her room there was a shelf full of all kinds of story books, that looked untouched.

"Yes" she answered, her face lighting up, and Jessica read her the story of Rumpelstilskin, using different tones of voice to make the story as expressive as possible. She noticed Bernie peeping at the door. When she was done, she kissed April goodnight and said loudly, so that Bernie listening at the door could hear too,

"I'll read you a story every night, if you behave a good girl...and you too Bernie, if you behave like a good boy." She heard scampering outside the door.
Mr. Bernstein arrived just as the children got into bed and so only had a few moments with them that day. Somehow Jessica felt that was planned.

****

"We'll pick you up tonight or else trust me, your day off won't start until after the kids leave for school tomorrow," Madge said to Jessica over the phone on Wednesday. Jessica noticed that Madge used the term 'kids' like Canadians do.
"Okay...but make it real late...sometimes the children don't fall asleep till about nine."
"Nine thirty then."
"Okay."

So at nine thirty Jessica was waiting at the end of the driveway for Madge and Willie. She'd had a rough day with Bernie. He went into her room that evening and had gotten into her cosmetics and ruined them all, making a holy mess all over the bed, dresser and floor. Mrs. Bernstein shrugged her shoulders when Jessica mentioned it to her. The door to her room could only be locked from inside, so if she wasn't there Bernie could easily get in and wreak havoc again. To prevent him from repeating this behavior, before she left, she placed most of her belongings into the clothes closet which was equipped with a lock. She moved the framed photographs from the dresser and put them in her suitcase, in the locked closet.

"Who they?" April asked her earlier that day, pointing to Josh and Jolene in the photograph.

"They're my sister's children…I'm their auntie," Jessica replied feeling like Judas, but it was a cardinal rule that under no circumstances should anyone - not even an innocent four year old - be told that she had children.

"What her name?" April asked, pointing to Jolene. Jessica told her.

"And he?"

"That's Joshua."

At nine fifty Madge and Willie pulled up.

"Don't tell me you've been waiting here since nine thirty," Willie said.

"I tried to get him to hurry," said Madge. "I told him if there's one Grenadian that's a stickler for time, it's you." Jessica smiled as she kissed them both and slid into the back seat with her carry-on bag, that she'd used on the plane and which had seen better days.

"Let me thaw out first, before I answer you."

Jessica and Madge went shopping the next day.

"Buy all the things you need," Madge encouraged her. "You can borrow some money from me until you get your paycheck."

It was a fun day. Jessica learned how to use the bus and enjoyed traveling on the metro. It was an adventure she couldn't wait to share with her children. She bought all the essential winter gear as well as writing material, an alarm clock, a weekend bag and new makeup.

"Since I might be waiting out in the cold for my good friends, I'd better be well prepared," she winked at Madge as she tried on a warm down filled coat.

"Not me...not me...blame Willie for being late last night," Madge responded, hiding her face with her hands and giggling.

They had lunch at a Chinese restaurant before returning home. Madge told Jessica all about the course credits she had earned by attending SGWU part-time. She encouraged Jessica to sign up as soon as the new term started again in September. I'll give you the names of some professors you'll do well to avoid, she said. They watched TV and relaxed and laughed. It was like the good old days again - when they were both growing up in Rockville.

Willie came home after his evening classes ended.

"It's snowing out there," he announced.

"Oh no!" exclaimed Madge. Jessica hastened to the window. This she had to see. It looked like thick white drops of rain catapulting downwards. It was exciting.

"We'd better take Jessica home, before the driving gets too bad," Willie advised. He didn't seem the least bit excited about the snow.

"I can take the bus," said Jessica. All of a sudden she was feeling adventurous and energized.

"Oh no...not with all these parcels," said Madge. "Next time but not tonight."

So after a light supper, they drove her home, and Jessica let herself in through the side entrance of the Bernstein's residence. Before she went in, she held her face up to the snow and sticking out her tongue, allowed a few snow flakes to alight on it in a cold but gentle caress.

CHAPTER 15

Grandma could hardly believe it. It was only Friday and Jacob came up the hill with a letter for her bearing a Canadian postage stamp. Jacob was used to going to the post office every day, with his satchel strung across his shoulder and opposite hip, to get the mail for the Bailey family. These came fast and furious. Mr. Bailey wrote home once or twice a month as did some of the other Bailey siblings. Flo and Madge were exceptional - they wrote home almost every week. Last week Ma Bailey proudly displayed Madge and Willie's wedding photographs to all neighbours and friends.

On the other hand, Grandma seldom went to the post office, as there had been no one to write to her. But now she joined that proud group of folks who had family 'abroad'.

"A leeetter fffor yooou, Maaa Hiiilly" Jacob said, as he reached into his satchel, very professionally, and brought out a pink envelope. Grandma was hanging wet clothes on a clothes line in the yard.

"Wo-o-y! A letter from Jessie already?...Thanks Jacob," said Grandma, both excited and happy. Leaving the bucket of clothes in the yard, she rushed inside to get her glasses. She had not stopped thinking of Jessica since she left last Saturday. How was the flight? Did she make it okay? How was the new job? Grandma hoped Jessica wasn't worrying too much about the children. She was just as attached to Jessica as she was to Audrey and she felt the same ache in her heart when Jessica left, as when Audrey passed away. As Pappy used to say, parting has its pangs. But she knew she had to be strong for the children just as she had to be strong for Jessica back then.

    She sat in the rocking chair on the verandah and read and reread the letter. Thank you Jesus, she whispered to herself when she was done, as she folded the letter and placed it in her bosom. When the twins arrived home from school, they sat on the bed together and she read it to them. She read it to Aunt Mattie that night and to Mrs. Bailey and to almost everyone who came by over the next week.

    She was going to reply to Jessica's letter that weekend, as soon as she had purchased some writing paper at the store. Jessica would be happy to hear that the twins were doing fine. They enjoyed the trip back from the airport in Mr. Farrow's car. She would be pleased to know that her father promised to come occasionally to carry the children to the beach along with Debbie and Trevor. She would tell her of the money Mr. Farrow put in her hands for the twins last Saturday. All in all he had turned out to be a decent man - despite what happened with Audrey years ago. It was a good thing she had kept her mouth shut about Audrey's illness...

    ****

It seemed that one week in Montreal was freezing cold and the next week without warning it turned blistering hot. The Bernstein children were off from school and in Jessica's care during July and August. They spent most of the day at a nearby summer camp, where they had passes to the swimming pool. Jessica also took swimming lessons, along with the children.

When she was not with the children at the pool, Jessica loved to sit in the backyard amidst the beautiful azaleas, geraniums, dahlias, petunias, roses and lilacs. It was the closest she felt to sitting on Grandma's verandah, in the shade of the flamboyant tree. She brought out her writing material and wrote children's stories and poems. Sometimes she simply wrote letters to her family and friends at home. Usually Bernie and April were with her and she would tell them stories or read to them. What a pity, she thought, that Mr. and Mrs. Bernstein seemed too busy to come out and enjoy this glorious place. She noticed that a gardener came once a week to cut the grass and work in the garden.

Mr. Bernstein seemed to be on the road a lot. When he was home, he was usually in the den. The only words Jessica could think of to describe him were 'dull and boring'. Mrs. Bernstein and Jessica gradually warmed towards each other. She was happy that Jessica seemed to have control of, and take such good care of the children. Jessica had made some progress with Bernie. In return for playing 'truck' and reading him stories, she actually got him to be more cooperative and less destructive. She had a calming influence on him.

Mrs. Bernstein told Jessica that many of Bernie's classmates were on medication to make them less rambunctious. When one little boy showed up at school one day without his medication, the principal had no choice but to go purchase it herself from the drug store and call his mother to come to the school and administer the medication. It was impossible for the teacher to conduct the class with the screams of this little boy.

Jessica recognised in Mrs. Bernstein, a nervous, frightened woman, who sought refuge in cigarettes. She smoked like a chimney, despite a bad case of smoker's cough. Jessica was sure she could put her finger on the root of the problem.

"That poor woman is living a lie," she confided in Madge one day. "And it's eating away at her." They were in Madge's kitchen making beef patties. Madge was all ears. "You know how many times that same fellow calls, asking for her?"

"Do you give her the messages?"

"Of course...every time. She says it's her butcher." Jessica smirked as she rolled out the dough with a rolling pin.

"Mmhmm?"

"She's always asking me...'Jessica, did the butcher call for me today?'" Jessica tried to imitate Mrs. Bernstein's throaty twang. Madge laughed, as Jessica continued. "If it's the butcher they sure have a lot of meat to talk about, because she's on the phone talking to him for hours on end."

"Where's the husband at these times?"

"I don't know...He's on the road maybe or at the office...I guess."

"Maybe they're both up to the same game."

"You know Madge...money doesn't always bring happiness."

"It can make life a damn lot easier though," answered Madge as she put a spoonful of cooked ground meat on each circle of dough.

"Okay, okay...you definitely need *some*." Using a fork, Jessica sealed the dough with the meat inside of it.

"I agree," said Madge spooning the last of the meat. She had to take some from circles that had too much and couldn't close properly. "It's a necessary but not sufficient ingredient for happiness."

During the summer, Mr. Bernstein's mother from New Brunswick paid her annual visit. Her son smiled indulgently at her but then left her up to her own devices. Mrs. Bernstein secretly referred to her as 'that old goat'. She had no rapport whatsoever with her grandchildren, whom she treated like little pests. She actually spoke more to Jessica than to anyone else in the house. Even so, she sometimes managed to put her whole foot in her mouth. Like that hot, humid day when she said to Jessica " I know now why those people who live in hot places are so lazy...I don't blame them." Jessica remained silent. *Lazy?...You've obviously never met my grandmother or my aunt...you old goat!*

During Mr. Bernstein's mother's visit, a formal dinner party was held in her honour. She spent all morning at the beauty parlor and then in the early afternoon attempted to nap with a bath towel rolled underneath her neck, trying not to mess up her expensive coiffure. She reminded Jessica of Albertine. That evening she out-dazzled everyone in her sparkling evening gown and impressive diamond jewelry.

More out of curiosity than anything else, Jessica agreed to help with the party. She wanted to get a close up view of how rich people partied. All the guests arrived punctually at seven thirty. Jessica was busy answering the door bell and taking wraps or shawls, if there were any. She marveled at the way many of them saw her as a robot or dummy standing at the door.

"Here...take this shawl" one woman said, while another simply deposited her stole on Jessica's outstretched arm. She felt invisible. She led them to the living room, where they met their hosts and had a pre-dinner cocktail of their choice.

Later, they were directed to the dining room, where they were treated to a multi-course meal on exquisite china. In between courses, the guests were entertained by a cellist. One old gentleman, with a handle bar mustache, sat next to Mr. Bernstein and laughed thunderously throughout the evening at everything Mr. Bernstein said. Another heavily made-up dame, with scarlet fingernails shrieked at the top of her voice for the benefit of everyone at the table it seemed. On the whole it was a dull and mirthless affair. Promptly at ten thirty everyone disappeared. It was as though a magician had waved his wand. Poof! The richly embossed invitations with gold lettering had stated the party was from seven thirty to ten thirty.

****

At the end of August, Mrs. Bernstein had Jessica remove all the children's clothes, that they had outgrown, from their closets and pack them up for a local charity.

"Feel free to take anything you wish," Mrs. Bernstein told Jessica. She had heard all about Jessica's niece and nephew in Grenada. Some of the items were almost brand new. Jessica helped herself to several pairs of Bernie's shorts and tee shirts, which both Josh and Jo could use. Too bad April is smaller than Jolene, she thought. When Mrs. Bernstein cleared out her own closet, Jessica salvaged several items that her grandmother could easily adjust for herself and Aunt Mattie.

So in addition to sending most of her small pay cheque home to Grandma, Jessica was proud to be able to send home a barrel at Christmas as well. She even included a few of Mr. Bernstein's shirts for Shark. Just to envision the excitement this barrel would cause in the household, made her happy. She was proud too of the fact that she had registered for two credit courses at SGWU. She immersed herself in her studies which she thoroughly enjoyed. Her social life was good. She became friendly with a few students at the university and also with some folks she met at church through Madge and Willie. She had no difficulty balancing work, studies and play.

****

Fleurina came from Toronto to spend Christmas with Madge and Willie. Jessica joined them late on Christmas eve after they had all returned from church.

"Look at you," said Flo. "You're back to your old skinny self." The last time she had seen Jessica was a month before the twins were born.

"Yes…I'm giving you good competition," replied Jessica laughingly. She showed Flo pictures of the twins and filled her in about their activities.

"My God…I can't believe they're this big already," remarked Flo.

They spoke about Ian and Albertine. Jessica was overjoyed that Ian's health seemed to be holding. She mentioned how attentive he was towards his grandchildren. Fleurina had written to Albertine from

England but never received a reply. "I think she's still mad at me for leaving," she said. "She didn't think I deserved a life of my own."

Jessica inquired about Chester.

"The school year finishes next August," Flo replied. "And as soon as that's done, he'll be joining me in Toronto."

Madge and Willie had a beautiful little Christmas tree on a table in the corner of the living room. Jessica carefully removed the Christmas gifts from her own bag and placed them with the others around the tree, adding to the festive aura of the apartment.

"Next year you guys have to come to Toronto for Christmas," Flo said.

They spent a cozy and happy Christmas together. After a sumptuous breakfast, the gifts were opened, amidst a lot of oohs and aahs. Throughout the day everyone chatted non-stop. There was so much catching up to be done. Flo told several humorous stories about her sojourn in England and her job at the hospital in Toronto. Madge and Willie divulged their plans to move to Ottawa the following summer while Jessica spoke of the children's stories and poems she was working on. She recalled those books she was subjected to in the public library when she was a child and decided even if she had to write them herself, her children were going to read stories where people like themselves were the heroes.

Later on, everyone chipped in to help with preparing the evening meal. It was Jessica's first Christmas away from her children. Despite all the festivity, all the joking around and chatting, she couldn't help wondering what Josh and Jo were doing and whether they were happy. She knew Grandma would do her very best for them. She had sent home gifts for everyone. "To be opened on Christmas day" a sticker on the packages read. Now it was Christmas day and they would have opened their presents. Were they laughing and cheerful and happy? Jessica hoped so.

****

On a bitterly cold day in the middle of January when the temperature dropped to below zero, Jessica went to meet April from the school bus. The bus arrived but there was no April. Bernie had graduated to a more advanced school by this time and took a different school bus. He was already at home. The bus driver said the first bus had broken down and all the children were transferred onto his bus.

"Was there a little girl left behind on the first bus?" She asked the bus driver.

"I don't think so," the bus driver answered but he promised to call up the bus depot and check. Jessica was very worried. In temperature like this, it only took a few minutes for any exposed skin to freeze.

She didn't know nor did she have the number where Mrs. Bernstein was but she did have the husband's number for emergencies. *And this is a big emergency.* Jessica telephoned Mr. Bernstein. He wasn't available, but she left a message that there was an emergency and he should call home urgently. She then called the school and spoke to the principal, who was very concerned. The principal promised to contact the bus company. Jessica was very disturbed. She knew that every minute counted. What should she do? She finally decided to call the police.

A big burly policeman dropped off April forty five minutes before Mrs. Bernstein arrived home. There was still no response from Mr. Bernstein. April had fallen asleep on the first school bus. When she awoke, the bus was parked at the depot. She pushed opened the door of the bus and got off. She decided to walk home, she said. The poor child was miles away from her home. Luckily a policeman spotted her and took her to the station. She told them her name and while they tried to find out who and where her parents were, they treated her to a big lollipop. She felt like a celebrity. A few minutes after, they received a call from a Jessica Farrow, who described the missing child they had in their custody.

There were phone calls back and forth when Mrs. Bernstein came home and found out what had occurred. Mr. Bernstein finally called home to check on the emergency. Lawyers got involved and there was talk of a law suit. Jessica never found out how it all ended. What was important to her was that April was safe. She realized how easily this incident could have had a tragic ending.

Since this occurrence Mrs. Bernstein seemed to value Jessica even more. She was always giving her gifts of shoes, purses, clothing or linen which Jessica appreciated very much. She put these items in the barrel that she was sending home for next Christmas. It was at this time Jessica asked for a letter of recommendation from Mrs. Bernstein. *I'd better strike while the iron is hot.*

****

Although Jessica was officially finished working for the Bernstein's after one year, she decided to accept Mrs.

Bernstein's offer to stay on for a further year, with a slight increase in salary. Mrs. Bernstein was ecstatic. Jessica felt that this was economically to her advantage, as she wouldn't have to undergo the big expenses involved in the rental and furnishing of an apartment. This would enable her to take another two credits at the university while at the same time allowing her to provide for her children and grandmother at home. She looked forward to increasing her small savings account too. In addition to this, she had developed an attachment to April and Bernie and even Mrs. Bernstein. One more year couldn't hurt, she thought.

Willie and Madge strongly advised her against this.

"Never mind how nice they seem girl…you always have to watch your back with these people."

"You should start looking for a better paying job and going on your own now," said Willie.

"It's only for one more year guys," Jessica tried to get them to see her point of view. Madge and Willie didn't try to persuade her further, especially since they were in the midst of their upcoming plans to move to Ottawa. Madge was getting a transfer to a branch of the Royal Bank in Ottawa and Willie was going to finish up his degree at Carleton university full time.

"Promise me you won't stay beyond this next year," Madge said to Jessica seriously.

"I promise," said Jessica. A few months later she bitterly regretted not following Willie and Madge's advice.

****

Grandma sensed that whenever cocoa and nutmeg prices were low, people felt less secure about their jobs. During these times, many people including public service employees, would often be laid off. Grenada had just entered such a period and rumour had it that opponents of the government were the first to be fired. She knew that Mrs. Gittens, who used to work with Jessica at the medical center, lost her job last week. Grandma was happy that Jessica was no longer working in that place.

Thank God she was getting a small cheque from Jessica every month. She didn't know how she would make ends meet otherwise. She hardly got any sewing jobs anymore. Jessica used to help with most of the sewing when she was here, but with the old eyes getting dimmer by the minute, Grandma could hardly see to even thread a needle these days. Then there was hardly anything coming in from her cocoa and nutmeg anymore. In the past, she and Mattie used to make a little money from the sale of these crops but now months were rolling by and not a red cent was coming in.

"Dis place goin' from bad to worse," she said to herself.

Another source of worry to Grandma was Shark. She wasn't quite sure of his whereabouts. It was simply impossible to get a straight answer out of him and useless to talk to his mother. But Grandma suspected he wasn't working at the hotel any longer. He was back to his old habit of hanging around *Percy's* and that Lucy woman, from down the road. Last week her husband came in the yard waving a cutlass, looking for Shark. He started shouting and using a lot of bad, curse words in front of the children. Even though Grandma assured him Shark wasn't at home, it didn't help. He threatened to chop them all up if Shark ever put foot in his house again. The children were badly frightened as was Grandma. She decided then and there to ask Terri Jones, Mrs. Bailey's eldest daughter, who lived in Grandville, to save a puppy for her the next time her Doberman had a litter.

"De sooner Jessica sen' for dese poor children, de better" she said to herself. "But in de meantime, we could use a good watch dog 'round here."

CHAPTER 16

When the senior Mrs. Bernstein visited during the second summer of Jessica's employment, Jessica declined the invitation to help with the annual party, even though she would have been paid a bit extra. By then she knew exactly what went on at these parties and could think of a host of other things she would rather do. Jessica was taking a summer course at SGWU and the last assignment had to be handed in the following week. She decided she would spend the time working on this assignment at the university library instead.

Mrs. Bernstein sr. was disappointed. She seemed a lot more needy on this visit. She begged Jessica to come upstairs and help her get into her new evening dress. Finally Jessica softened. She went to Mrs. Bernstein's room at seven o' clock and zipped her into her new, black, sequined gown.

"Could you fasten these please?" The old lady had finally learned to use the word *Please* to Jessica. Jessica fastened the beautiful diamond necklace, which she recognized from last year, around Mrs. Bernstein's thick neck with matching bracelet around the wrist of her speckled arm.

"Now which pair of shoes do you think is more suitable?" Mrs. Bernstein brought out a pair of black satin shoes as well as higher heeled gold and silver ones from the closet. Jessica advised her on the latter, since she would be sitting down for most of the evening. Finally with nothing else left for her to do or give advice on, Jessica told Mrs. Bernstein how stunning she looked, which is what Jessica thought she wanted to hear and leaving her admiring herself in front of a full length mirror, returned downstairs.

The bus pulled up as the guests were showing up at the Bernstein's residence. Jessica entered the bus and sat about four seats back from the driver. She had learned to choose her seats with more caution after the time when she sat in the front seat closest to that nosy driver, who tried to get all her business out of her. "Where're you from? Where do you work? Where're you off to?" were some of the questions he inquisitively pestered her with.

Jessica missed not having Willie and Madge in Montreal. She had helped them move to Ottawa two weekends ago. The last thing Madge said to her when they wished each other goodbye was,

"Promise me girl, after this year you're leaving those Bernsteins."

"I promise" said Jessica, hugging her friend. "And will you promise me to take good care of that little bun in the oven?" Madge laughed. Jessica suspected that the fatigue Madge was experiencing recently was due to nothing else but a pregnancy.

"Yes, Ma Hilly" replied Madge, implying that Jessica had taken on some of the qualities of her perceptive grandmother.

Jessica felt a sense of contentment. All in all it was a good year and a half at the Bernstein's residence. Mrs. Bernstein was very kind and generous to her. With all the second hand items she had given her, Jessica's barrel for home this Christmas was almost ready. Many women, who came from the Caribbean to work as domestics, didn't have it half as good as she did. In fact she'd heard of some real horror stories. But Jessica was lucky and she was so grateful. By the end of April next year, she should have completed the first year at university towards a Bachelor's degree. That would be no mean accomplishment and should certainly help her to secure a well paying job, perhaps with the Government or with a big company somewhere.

Jessica left the library at closing time, happy that her assignment was completed to her satisfaction. She took the bus back home. The party was over and the guests were long gone by the time she arrived at home. While still on the bus, she retrieved the keys from her hand bag, in preparation for letting herself in through the side entrance, as usual.

"There she is...now hand over that ring at once," Jessica heard Mrs. Bernstein sr. shout. Jessica blinked. *Who was Mrs. Bernstein yelling at?* She wondered what was going on. She shut the side door behind her and turned the latch.

"Where is my diamond ring, Jessica?" Mrs. Bernstein sr. was actually talking to Jessica as she walked closer to her, looking at her accusingly. Mr. and Mrs. Bernstein looked on from behind the old lady.

"Whaat?" stammered Jessica, in total confusion. She looked from one face to the other as she turned around.

"What did you do with my diamond ring you took from my jewelry box earlier today?" said Mrs. Bernstein sr.
Is this some kind of sick joke? "Pardon me, Mrs. Bernstein but I don't know what you're talking about," Jessica answered with a frown.

"Yeah…sure." Mrs. Bernstein sr. answered sarcastically. "I'm talking about my diamond ring. The one you stole from my jewelry box."

"Mrs. Bernstein, I did not take or steal a diamond ring or anything whatsoever from your jewelry box today or any other day." Jessica spoke slowly and deliberately as she looked again from one face to the other. *Why the hell is the young Mrs. Bernstein not saying a single word in my defense?*
Mr. Bernstein cleared his throat and stuck his hands awkwardly in the side pockets of his trousers.

"I'm sorry Jessica" he said, looking very uncomfortable "but my mother claims that her diamond ring, which was in her jewelry box, has disappeared. Since you were the only other person…"
Jessica totally lost it at this point.

"I don't give a rat's behind what your mother claims, Mr. Bernstein," she shouted at him. "I already said I don't know anything about any damn ring." Then looking into the old lady's face, she said "I don't know what tricks you are up to. You begged me to come up to help you dress today…and now you pull this?"
The young Mrs. Bernstein went into a fit of coughing while the blood seemed to have drained from the face of Mrs. Bernstein sr.

"Thief!" she shouted at Jessica. Then turning to her son she said "Marty, she probably rushed out to pawn it."

"You're sick," Jessica hissed. "Sick and crazy."

Her whole world was crashing down around her. She felt as though she was free falling from a cloud or plane and didn't know how, when or where she was going to land. She stormed down the hallway, down the stairs and into her bedroom. She was astounded at the sight that awaited her there. The room had been ransacked. All the items that Mrs. Bernstein had given her, which she was planning to send home were all over the floor and bed. Her clothes and other belongings were scattered all over as well. The photographs on her dresser were knocked down and their glass frames were broken. The little container in which she kept her jewelry was taken out and emptied. Her suitcase had been removed from the top shelf of the closet and the jewelry box with the golden J bracelet was gaping open.

"Oh my God!" cried Jessica. She felt completely violated. *How dare they!*

"I'm afraid" said Mr. Bernstein, coming down the stairs behind Jessica, "I'm going to have to call the cops...as that ring was valued at well over one hundred thousand dollars."
Jessica could hardly believe her ears. *Which arsehole buys a stupid ring for a hundred thousand dollars?* She pointed to the mess in her room.

"Who did this?" she asked. Mr. Bernstein declined to answer.

"Go ahead Mr. Bernstein...call the damn cops."

****

At one a.m. the phone rang in Madge and Willie's Ottawa apartment. Willie reached over to the night table and grabbed it.

"Hello," he answered.

"Willie...it's Jessica." Why was Jessica calling at this ungodly hour? Willie bolted upright in bed. It had to be an emergency. He thought he heard sobbing.

"What's the matter, Jess?" he asked concerned.

"Jess? Did you say Jess?" Madge was awake and sitting upright in bed now.

"They said I stole a diamond ring," Jessica blurted out between sobs. "And they've called the police." Between frequent bouts of sobbing, Jessica managed to get the whole sordid story out to Willie, who repeated it to Madge.

"Take several pictures of the mess they made in your room, Jess," Willie advised. "And tell the police you will not talk to them without your lawyer present." Before the hour was up, a young Montreal criminal lawyer - a friend of Willie and Madge - was contacted and agreed to help Jessica.

When the police arrived, Jessica declined from answering any questions, stating she would do so only in the presence of her lawyer. She did however, state that she would herself like to press charges of vandalism and violation of privacy. She showed them the condition of her room, which she had not touched, pointing out the broken items. She kept her copy of the police report for her lawyer.

Jessica moved out of the Bernstein household the next day, when Willie arrived with Curtis Lincoln, his lawyer friend. She did not sleep a wink that night. She locked herself in her room and packed all her belongings, leaving behind the gifts from the generous Mrs.

Bernstein. She left them as she found them, strewn all over the room. She didn't say goodbye to anyone. She gave the house key to the lawyer. He returned it to Mrs. Bernstein as he sat with her at the dinette table.

Mrs. Bernstein's face looked puffy and she seemed to be going through more cigarettes than usual. She kept her eyes averted and did not attempt to speak to Jessica. The children had left for camp earlier that morning. They must have sensed something was askew when their mother instead of Jessica gave them their breakfast. Jessica stayed in her room until Willie arrived. She remembered Madge's advice about trusting these people. She never thought it would happen to her. *I should have listened to Madge and Willie.*

****

Something was not quite right. Grandma had not received a decent letter from Jessica in three weeks. She was used to hearing from Jessica every single week, sometimes twice in the same week. Jessica would often write simple letters to the twins, now that they were learning to read. Often she would enclose short stories or poems for them. But three weeks had passed and there had been no letter from her. Even the children noticed and the first thing they asked when they came from school, was if there was a letter from Mummy. Grandma got a card on her birthday with a cheque in it, and Jessica had scribbled a little note saying that she was no longer at the Bernstein's and all letters to her, should be sent in care of Madge.

That didn't make any sense at all. In the letter Grandma received three days before the card, Jessica was praising the Bernsteins and talking about taking more courses at the university. And didn't Madge and Willie not move to Ottawa? Something was definitely wrong and Jessica was not telling her about it. But Madge must know and if Madge knew, then her mother must also know.

The rain was drizzling. The wind was increasing in intensity. Grandma slipped on her rubber boots and raincoat of sturdy plastic bags that she had stitched together and hurried down the hill to talk to Ethel Bailey.

"You hear from Madge lately, Ethel?" she asked her.

"Yes...I hear from her today."

"What's de latest?" Grandma thought she would see if Mrs. Bailey would offer the information willingly, without her trying to play detective and pry it out of her.

"She say as soon as she and Willie get settled in Ottawa, she gwine start de papers for Julian to go up to Canada."

"Mmhmm...dat's good."

"Julian so happy he could burst," smiled Mrs. Bailey. She was about to repeat a long discourse about her youngest child, passing both O and A Level exams and now going to Canada but Grandma decided to cut straight to the point.

"She mention anyt'ing 'bout Jessica?"

"In her las' letter...not de one today...she mention Jessica stayin' wid dem for ah little while...she not at de place she been workin' anymore."

"She din say why?"

"No...but Jessica could leave after de year, you know...some gyurls leave before dat and get other jobs. Madge start workin' in de bank after..."

"Yeah…yeah," said Grandma and stood up to go back up the hill. That Ethel thought herself the expert on all the girls in Canada now, she said to herself. "I better run before dat big shower of rain come down."

Ethel Bailey obviously didn't have anything to add to what Grandma already knew. Well, she was going to ask Jessica outright. She didn't like this hide and seek game at all. That night after the twins were asleep, Grandma got out her glasses, took out her pen and writing paper from her trunk and wrote a serious letter to Jessica.

****

The pre-trial hearing was set for September 4th. Curtis Lincoln, Jessica's lawyer, was confident that the judge was going to throw the Bernstein case out of court. After talking with him, her assurance was boosted.

"First of all there is no evidence that this ring the lady describes even existed. She has no receipts, pictures, nothing at all" the lawyer assured her.

"Mr. Bernstein said the ring was valued at well over one hundred thousand dollars."

"They couldn't produce any evidence of this. There was a bracelet valued at one hundred and eighty thousand but no ring."

"Oh?"

"Then if it did indeed exist, did she bring it to her son's home? Did anybody see it at all? No…only this eighty year old very forgetful and needy lady, who couldn't even get dressed by herself for the party. She begged you to assist her in getting dressed."

Jessica hadn't thought of this line of reasoning and was quite pleased.

"And if somebody stole it...what proof do they have that it was you? They'll have to prove that. After all, one is innocent until proven guilty. Not the other way around."

Jessica nodded.

"Plus there was a party in the house that day...and the children were also there," Mr. Lincoln continued.

Jessica was feeling better by the minute.

"And if they even attempt character assassination, I'm ready for them," the lawyer said with a slight chuckle. Jessica had given him the glowing letter of recommendation Mrs. Bernstein had written for her less than six months ago.

By the time their case was called much later in the day than they expected, Jessica was suffering from a terrible headache. She looked around but did not see any of the Bernsteins present. The judge was a stern, tubby little man, with no neck to separate his head from his torso. He appeared to be as old as Mrs. Bernstein sr.

The prosecution laid out its case, stating how very good and generous Mr. and Mrs. Bernstein and Mrs. Bernstein sr. were to Jessica. She was allowed free reign of the house. They showered her with all kind of gifts but then she got too greedy. She decided to bite the hand that fed her. In her usual friendly way, Mrs. Bernstein sr. paid Jessica the honour and invited her upstairs while she was dressing for her annual high fashion party. When she opened her jewelry box to take out her diamond necklace and bracelet, which Jessica fastened for her, Jessica most certainly saw the diamond ring and decided to steal it. It is a fact that the ring was there before Jessica arrived and was absent after she left.

Jessica felt like she was having a bad dream from which she would wake up soon. She couldn't believe her ears. The prosecution made her appear like a charity case - as if the Bernsteins were sooo kind and generous to her for absolutely nothing in return. *Bullshit!* However she was sure her sharp thinking lawyer would handle this effectively.

The defense lawyer got up to speak.

"My Lord…" He began. Before he could get another word out, the old judge shouted,

"Shut up and sit down. Your client is nothing but a disgusting thief. She should be incarcerated." Jessica felt as though her head were about to explode.

"Excuse me My Lord but…"

"Mr. Lincoln…I said to shut up and sit down or I'll hold you in contempt of court." The old judge was screaming now. Mr. Lincoln hesitated for a moment, then sat down.

"Crazy old bastard," he said to Jessica underneath his breath. *Is this what goes on in a court of law and justice?* So instead of the case being thrown out of court, a trial date was set for February of the following year.

CHAPTER 17

Late that night, Jessica caught the last bus back to Ottawa from Montreal. Despite a traumatic day, she was hopeful and light spirited. Maybe it was because of all that wine she had drunk. Or maybe it was the good company. After leaving the court house, her lawyer took her out to dinner at a fancy restaurant. He told her that he would make sure the judge trying the actual case in February, would not be this same old geezer, who was notorious for these illogical outbursts.

"He's senile and crazy," Curtis Lincoln said.

"Then why is he still there…why hasn't he retired?" Jessica wanted to know.

"Retire?…You can remain a judge until the minute you drop dead," Curtis replied.

"It seems to me that justice is not a priority then…"

Curtis smiled, as the waiter approached with the wine. Jessica noticed that when he smiled, his whole face changed. When she'd first met Curtis Lincoln, he reminded her of the TV character, Colombo. All she saw was his ill fitting, droopy rain coat but now she noticed he had kind, sensitive eyes and sparkling, white teeth.

After being served, he held his glass aloft and looking directly at Jessica, said;

"Cheers to success."

"Cheers," responded Jessica and they touched glasses. They both took a sip. Curtis continued.

"Let's put it this way…the system here is not the best but it could be a whole lot worse."

"That's easy to say when you're not the one on the receiving end of the boot," answered Jessica.

But Curtis Lincoln had been on the receiving end of the boot before. Jessica learned that evening that Curtis was the son of a Jamaican father and Nova Scotian mother. He himself was born in Montreal. He recounted his childhood in Montreal, when coloured children were not allowed to use the swimming pool at the center town YMCA. He recalled going into a restaurant on Sherbrooke street, with a group of his school friends and being told "we don't serve coloured people here." He told numerous stories of working on the railroad, which is how he paid his tuition for law school, and encountering customers that were down right nasty and racist.

It was a source of sadness to Curt that neither of his parents lived long enough to see him complete law school. His parents were both in their late forties when he was born. He was their 'miracle' baby. Yes, if anyone had earned the right to talk of the boot - it was Curtis Lincoln. Jessica looked at him with new found respect. Despite it all, he had succeeded. He never ceased to, as Aunt Mattie would say, stand tall.

****

Mrs. Bernstein and her lawyer agreed with Curtis Lincoln to give Jessica six months pay in exchange for dropping the vandalism and privacy charges. Although six months salary without the advantage of room and board was hardly worth anything, Jessica was pleased.

She checked the daily papers and was out there every day job hunting, but hadn't found anything yet and was fast depleting her small savings. She also had to send the usual money order home to Grandma. Even though Madge and Willie insisted that she didn't have to, Jessica was determined to contribute to the household expenses. She didn't want to be a burden on them. After all, Willie was now at Carleton full time and Madge was pregnant. It was heartwarming that once again her friends had come through for her. Going back and forth to Montreal from Ottawa, was an additional expense she hadn't bargained on. Thank God she didn't register for courses at SGWU yet, as she would have certainly lost the deposit. So when Curtis called her up about the small settlement, Jessica was relieved.

"Great Curt" she exclaimed. "That will be so helpful."

In the foyer of the building, Madge picked up the mail from the mailbox on her way up to their fifth floor apartment, that afternoon. There was a letter for Jessica from her grandmother. Jessica was expecting it. She knew from experience that she could only keep Grandma in the darkness for so long. She was hoping that the pendulum would have swung back to the right side and she would have something positive to say when she wrote. But now she had to bite the bullet. She opened the envelope.

My darling Jessica, what going on with you? I know something wrong and you not telling me what it is. Talk about cutting straight to the point - that was Grandma. *In one letter you say how nice Mrs. Bernstein is to you and the next letter say you not there anymore. You gone quite in Ottawa to live with Madge and Willie. What happen Jessica? I know something happen, so just write and tell me whatever it is. I waiting.* As usual without being told a word, Grandma had figured out that something was wrong. That lady should have been a detective. She could smell a rat from a zillion miles away.

    Jessica had asked Madge not to mention a word about this incident in letters back home. Not even to Flo, who had called last week to say Chester had arrived in Toronto from England. Apart from the embarrassment of the accusation, she didn't want her grandmother to get too worried. But sometimes silence can be more deafening. Jessica knew she had to write her grandmother right away and tell her everything that was going on.

    She had one other piece of business to take care of first. It was urgent and she dreaded it. She had to contact Mrs. Bernstein about her mail. Grandma had asked whether she received the cards that the children made for her birthday, which were mailed to her at the Bernstein's. She would like to say in her reply that they were at least on the way. She would have to give Mrs. Bernstein a forwarding address, which she had deliberately not done before. She wanted to sever all ties. She didn't want any contact with that treacherous household anymore. Or, a better idea came to her mind, she would ask Curt to go by and collect her mail.

    Jessica picked up the phone and dialed the Bernstein's number in Montreal. For the next two hours she got nothing but the busy signal. *She must be talking with her butcher.* Then finally at about seven o'clock a raspy voice answered.

"Hello?"

"Mrs. Bernstein...this is Jessica."

"Jessica?...oh my God...Jessica?!" she sounded pleased to hear from Jessica. "I've been wanting to contact you...but I didn't have your number."

Jessica remained very businesslike.

"I think you have some mail there for me, Mrs. Bernstein and I..."

Mrs. Bernstein jumped in before Jessica could finish what she was saying.

"Jessica...are you working yet?"

None of your damn business. She ignored the question.

"If you don't mind, Mrs. Bernstein...I'll ask Mr. Lincoln to pass by the house..."

"Jessica...we miss you so much...the children miss you...this was all a big mistake," Mrs. Bernstein rambled on. Jessica remained silent. *After all you people put me through, now you call it just a 'big mistake?'* But then what Mrs. Bernstein said next, caused her to sit upright and stutter,

"Whaaat? What did you say, Mrs. Bernstein?"

"Yes my dear...the old goat found the ring in her jewelry box when she returned to her home. She never brought it here at all."

Madge came out from the bedroom when she heard Jessica squealing. "What's going on?" she asked with her gestures.

"They've found the ring?!" Jessica repeated, both to Mrs. Bernstein and to Madge. The tears were pouring down her cheeks. She felt like a weight had suddenly been lifted from her shoulders. Madge clapped her hands with joy.

"Do the lawyers know about this?"

"Marty said not to say anything yet…but since you called…" Mrs. Bernstein stopped to clear her throat, then continued. "Since you called, I thought I'd let you know."

"Thanks very much, Mrs. Bernstein…that's excellent news …and my lawyer will be by to talk with you."

"Jessica…" But Jessica was crying too much, she didn't hear a thing that Mrs. Bernstein was saying. She simply mumbled,

"Bye…" and hung up the receiver.

****

Madge had been having severe abdominal cramps since the early morning. She decided to call in sick from work. By mid-afternoon when Jessica returned from a job interview, Madge was doubled over in pain. Jessica called a taxi and took her to the emergency department of the General hospital. She wrote a note leaving a message at home for Willie.

By the time Willie arrived at the hospital, Madge had already aborted the foetus and was scheduled for a D&C the following morning.

"It was not meant to be," he said sadly to Jessica. He looked so distressed that Jessica couldn't think of a single word of consolation to say to him. She just held his hand and squeezed it. She thought of her own pregnancy, almost seven years ago, when she had wished something like this would happen to her. As ungrateful as she was, God had given her a double blessing. She wished that Madge and Willie would one day be blessed in that way too.

She left the couple together and to pass the time walked down to the cafeteria. On the way she stopped to read a notice board, where several job vacancies were posted. She made note of many of them that she would definitely apply for. There were a few clerical positions in the lab, which seemed more appealing, the more she thought about them.

Jessica remained at the hospital with Madge that night. She insisted that Willie go home and get some rest. The next day after Madge's surgery, Willie drove them both back home, before he returned to Carleton.

"Don't worry," Madge said to him. "I'm going to be fine…and I'm sure we're going to have another chance." Willie kissed her gently on the cheek. He seemed a lot more distraught than Madge was.

"I'm glad I didn't say anything to Mammie yet," Madge said to Jessica when Willie left.

****

Grandma received a letter from Jessica and was relieved. But she was angry at those damn Bernstein people for calling her granddaughter a thief. They really didn't know who they were dealing with. They're lucky that she couldn't just take the bus and go pay them a visit - else they would have gotten a piece of her mind. She would have let them have it. "Who de hell dem t'ink dey is? Tellin' lie like dat on me poor grandaughter. De senile old witch leave she ring home and den say Jessica t'ief it." She could imagine just how hurt Jessica was through all this. But thank God, she didn't crumble. At times like these you need to ask God for courage and strength and sooner or later you're bound to come through.

Grandma went to the kitchen as she lightheartedly began to hum a familiar tune. She was going to bake a nice coconut bun now. Mr. Farrow was coming on Sunday to take the twins to the beach, along with his own children. They were looking forward to the outing so much. Josh had darkened up quite a lot and his legs were beginning to stretch out. He was going to be quite tall. He looked a lot like Jessica now. Sometimes if she looked at Jolene a certain way, she saw Pappy. It was funny how in later generations the old features repeated themselves.

Grandma was going to ask Mr. Farrow to take some pictures of them with Jessica's camera. She never learned how to work the silly thing and she didn't want to ask Shark for any favours. She knew Jessica would be overjoyed to get pictures of the children for Christmas. Maybe she would even get Mattie to spruce up herself to have her picture taken. Then there was Spice, the new puppy, that the children doted over - she must send Jessica a picture of Spice too.

****

Jessica could hardly believe her ears. Curtis Lincoln was certainly coming through for her. He met with the Bernstein's lawyer today, he said, and together they agreed on an out-of-court settlement. The figure Mr. Lincoln was quoting sounded too good to be true, to Jessica.

She had been worrying about Christmas fast approaching and not having anything to send home this year. There was no way on earth that she would accept a single thing from that Mrs. Bernstein again - not even a pin. She'd had enough of that kind of generosity - the kind that stabs you in the back later. But if she was hearing what Curt was saying correctly, she had just hit the jackpot. Visions of a new bathroom for Grandma, a refrigerator and gas stove in the kitchen floated in front of her eyes.

"They agreed to this?" Jessica fought to keep back the excitement. She felt like jumping up and down and screaming at the top of her voice.

"Yes," said Curtis. "They realized if we went to court, it would be much worse for them."

The phone rang again almost immediately as Jessica hung up from talking with Curtis. It was the General hospital. She had gone for an interview two days ago and they were offering her a position, to start the following week. They wanted her to come in the next day, to fill up forms and sign papers. Jessica was intoxicated with happiness. She had to call Madge at work to give her the good news. Now she was envisioning much, much, more - she would be able to fulfill her dream at last and bring her children to Canada.

That night at supper, Willie and Madge brought Jessica back down to earth.

"You can't send for the kids now," Madge said.

"Why not?"

"You should wait until you get citizenship before you apply for them to come up," said Willie.

"But that won't be for another three to four years."

"Jessie…we didn't tell you this…but you remember my friend Nora Spencer?"

"Yes…I remember her."

"She came up on the domestic scheme too," continued Madge. "She wrote on her papers that she didn't have any children…and five years later when she applied to bring up her children, guess what…"
Willie looked at Madge who stopped for a moment to control tears that threatened. He continued for her,
"They deported her…just last week she had to leave the country."
Jessica pushed away her plate. She wasn't hungry anymore. She couldn't believe this. That little lie she had to tell was catching up with her - biting her in the heart where it hurts the most.

CHAPTER 18

Cyprian Bailey had finally retired after forty years of working abroad. First in Panama and the U.S., then Curacao, then for the last thirty years he worked on an ocean liner in the Atlantic. Mrs. Bailey said all the children were grown up now and it was time for him to come home and rest.

He did anything but rest. First of all he redid their entire kitchen. Secondly he built an extension to the house - two more bedrooms and a modern bathroom - for when the children and grandchildren visited, Ethel Bailey said. Although no one said anything outright to her, everyone in Rockville was envious of Mrs. Bailey's good fortune.

"Now dat most of de children gone…what dey need such a big-house for?"

"I hear Julian, de las' boy, goin' soon."

"Cyprian gettin' on like he possessed," one neighbour remarked.

"Never mind…I wish I could a' get me husband to move he backside like she own oui."

Grandma heard the envy in the voices that made these comments. When you do a good job, sometimes you make it look easy. For forty years Ethel Bailey raised her family alone - her husband was away most of the time. She had her ups and she had her downs. That business with Dawson was one of the downs, and Mattie never could forgive her for that. She spoke as though Dawson was an innocent little baby that Ethel corrupted. But where was that Dawson now? It's not as though Ethel caused him to abandon his wife and child. Grandma shook her head and muttered to herself, "Yeah Lord…every pig have a Saturday."

****

Ian came up the hill, the same time as Cyprian was talking to Grandma about a project Jessica had written to him about. Spice barked ferociously, sensing the presence of a newcomer in the yard.

"Okay Spice…okay Spice," Grandma quieted her down with her soothing voice.

"What a big bark she's got already," Ian commented. He joined Cyprian and Grandma on the verandah. Grandma noticed the familiar pink envelope in his shirt pocket. Jessica had arranged for him, he said, to get a new refrigerator for Grandma as well as flush toilet, sink, ceramic tiles and other fixtures for a brand new bathroom. Cyprian was to add an extension to the back of the building to house this new room. This was Jessica's Christmas gift and she wanted the work done urgently.

"That Jessica!" Grandma shook her head, but deep down she was excited and proud. The children heard the adults talking and were excited too.

"Wo-o-o-oy!" they shouted, as they jumped around the house playing with Spice.

Josh and Jolene couldn't get home fast enough from school every afternoon. They followed Mr. Bailey around as he and a few other workmen made cement blocks and sawed and measured and installed and plastered and painted. He allowed the children to help him with some minor jobs and they were thrilled. Joshua enjoyed helping to make concrete blocks, while Jolene preferred painting. Mr. Bailey had to break down part of the back wall of the kitchen and reposition the back kitchen window to accommodate this new addition. Finally the new bathroom was finished. It was beautiful.

In the dining room, carefully positioned so that it could be seen from the verandah, stood a brand new refrigerator. So thanks to Jessica, Grandma could now offer a cold drink with ice to visitors. Those neighbours, who had not yet moved up that rung on the social ladder, were welcome to get ice from Grandma's fridge.

****

Jessica enjoyed her work at the laboratory. She received and prepared the specimens for the different labs. She sent out reports, answered the phones and generally did a multitude of tasks. She learned about Hemolytic Disease of the Newborn - how antibodies formed by the mother could attack a foetus with the corresponding antigen. The most common of these antibodies was known as Anti-D in the Rh group and to prevent the body from forming them, a prophylactic dose was now routinely given to Rh negative women after they gave birth. She wondered whether Aunt Mattie had formed Rh antibodies which caused her to lose six babies before

Shark was born. Maybe Shark was the only Rh negative foetus.

Jessica appreciated being busy. Her days flew by. Her schedule included working some weekends, which meant she had some weekdays off. It was great 'going against the grain' as she put it. She took evening classes at Carleton university and sometimes she would meet Willie and some other friends, if they had late classes on that day.

That winter, she moved into a condominium apartment on the East side of Ottawa. Even though she was disappointed at not being able to bring up the children yet, she decided to use the settlement Curtis had gotten her, to pay down on an apartment. That way she had an asset that was appreciating in value. She enjoyed furnishing her apartment and making drapes for the huge French windows. On the walls of her bedroom were blown up pictures of Josh and Jolene, Grandma with her arms around Josh and Jo with Spice, and her Dad at the beach with Trevor and Debbie. She'd been overjoyed to receive these from home last Christmas. Grandma said she was sorry she couldn't send a picture of Aunt Mattie and her son but she would get one soon to send for Jessica. She would send her a picture of the new bathroom as soon as it was finished too.

Grandma didn't make too much fuss about Jessica spending her money on something as unnecessary as a new bathroom. In fact, she seemed to participate actively in the design. She found it impractical, she said, to have the shower stall in the same room as the toilet.

"What if somebody have to go de same time as somebody else using de shower?" she wanted to know.

Jessica chuckled to herself and instructed Mr. Bailey to separate the two units, if that was what Grandma preferred.

****

Curtis surprised Jessica with a beautiful dried floral arrangement for her living room. He'd called one Friday while he was in Ottawa on business. Jessica invited him over for supper later that evening.

"Don't wear anything fancy…as I haven't got any furniture in here yet…you'll be sitting on the carpet." Then she called Madge and Willie.

"Curt is coming over," she said. "So why don't you guys come over too…I'm going to make some callaloo soup."

"I'm not feeling that great today," Madge declined the invitation. "I'm looking forward to going to bed early." But when she hung up the receiver, she winked at Willie, "Let's give Curt some time to make his move."

On her way home from work, Jessica picked up some salted pigs' tails, green bananas, yams, sweet potato and callaloo from a West Indian market down town. She made callaloo soup for two. Her soup was sizzling on the stove by the time Curtis arrived. He was almost hidden by the huge floral arrangement he was carrying, when Jessica opened the door.

"Something smells good" he said, entering the apartment. He offered her the huge bouquet.

"For me?" she said. "It's beautiful." She took the flowers from him.

"Beautiful flowers for a beautiful lady," he replied with that charming smile of his. Jessica was touched. She put the flowers down near the French windows in the living room and returned to help Curt with his coat and overshoes. She hung the coat in the closet.

"Another little gift" Curtis said, as he picked up from the floor, something he had rested there while he got his coat and overshoes off. "Here."
It was a chilled bottle of wine in a gift bag.

"Thank you," grinned Jessica and went to the kitchen to put the wine in the refrigerator. *What a charming guy!* When she returned Curt was holding an envelope towards her.

"Not another gift" said Jessica, looking baffled.

"No…no" replied Curtis, laughing. "This is a letter Mrs. Bernstein asked me to give to you."

Curtis admired Jessica's apartment, then they sat at the little table in the kitchen drinking wine and eating callaloo soup.

"It's delicious" Curt said, biting on a piece of salted pigs' tail. "I've never had this before."

"I think it's a specialty of the southern Caribbean region" Jessica remarked.

"It's more like a stew," Curt answered.

Afterwards they sat on large floor cushions in the living room. She felt very comfortable with Curt. She read the letter from Mrs. Bernstein, while he looked at her picture album.

"Who are these lovely children?" Curt asked as he turned the pages of her album.

"These are my twins," she answered. It was the very first time she was talking about her children to anyone who didn't already know about them. "This is Joshua and here is Jolene, with Spice." He saw pictures taken at the Bailey's beach picnic years ago. "This is Grandma and Ma Bailey, Madge's mother."

"Madge is the spitting image of her Mum," he commented.

"And this is my Dad and Trevor and Debbie, my little brother and sister."

Curtis looked at the entire picture album, admiring the unique beauty of Grenada, with its magnificent St. George's harbour, gorgeous white sand beaches, luscious vegetation and mountainous terrain, at the same time learning about Jessica's family and close friends.

"Mr. and Mrs. Bernstein have split up," said Jessica putting the letter back into its envelope.

"Yes...I know," replied Curt. He had heard about the messy divorce, but right now he had something more important on his mind. He returned to the pages with Josh and Jo and said to Jessica,

"And where is the children's father now?"

"He's in England," Jessica replied. "He left for England before the twins were born."

"So he's never seen them?"

"No," Jessica replied.

"But he must have pictures...."

"Since that evening I told him I was pregnant, Jack and I have never spoken or written a single word to each other." Jessica took a sip from her glass of wine. It seemed like a century had passed since that memorable evening at the ice cream parlor.

"He doesn't even help to support them?" Jessica smiled.

"Support them?...He's married with three or four other children now."

"That's unbelievable."

Curtis shook his head as he looked across at Jessica. He realized just what a fighting spirit she must have. She had survived more than one knock out punch in her life and seemingly without bitterness or hostility. She was definitely an extraordinary person.

CHAPTER 19

A few weeks after Curt's visit, Jessica called the number that Mrs. Bernstein had written in the letter to her. To her surprise, Mrs. Bernstein wanted to meet her in person.

"I don't have the time," Jessica told her. "What with work and school...it's just not possible."

"Please Jessica...just for a few minutes," Mrs. Bernstein implored. It reminded Jessica of that time when Mrs. Bernstein sr. had begged her to come up to her room. She was accused of stealing a diamond ring after that. Well, she certainly wasn't going to make the same mistake twice.

"Sorry but I'm not coming to Montreal anytime soon... I don't have the time." Jessica was firm.

"Oh no...you don't have to come to Montreal...I'll come to Ottawa," Mrs. Bernstein said, taking Jessica completely by surprise. *She probably wants to see where I live.* Jessica changed tactics.

"Okay...why don't we meet for lunch at Sparks restaurant, in the Byward market?" They agreed on a date and time, which on two occasions Jessica had to cancel. Finally the day had come. It was a cold and dreary Thursday and Jessica was off work, having worked the previous weekend.

At eleven thirty, she went to meet Mrs. Bernstein for lunch at the restaurant. Mrs. Bernstein was already seated at a table for two near the window when Jessica arrived. It was in the non-smoking section.

"Hello," she stood up to embrace Jessica, who was about to offer her hand. Jessica returned the embrace.

"How are you?" she asked. Mrs. Bernstein looked gaunt. Jessica was surprised to see the gray showing through in her hair. This lady didn't even know the natural colour of her hair anymore.

"You look great, Jessica."

"Thanks…and how are the children?"

"They're doing fine" she answered, but in her eyes there was an undeniable look of sadness.

After the waitress brought them their entrees then left to serve other customers, Mrs. Bernstein reached across the table and took Jessica's hand.

"Jessica…I want to apologize to you," she said. Jessica looked at her. Mrs. Bernstein continued. "We treated you so badly and I want to apologize from the bottom of my heart. You were so kind, so good, so honourable…"

"I have already put all that behind me," Jessica replied. "But thank you, I appreciate your apology." Jessica squeezed her hand slightly.

"I found this little poem that Bernie and April said you wrote and used to read for them." Mrs. Bernstein released Jessica's hand and fumbled around in her *Gucci* purse. She pulled out a pink envelope with a pink sheet of writing paper that Jessica easily recognized. She had originally written that poem for her own children but used to read it to the Bernstein children whenever she felt they had a rough day at school or were experiencing some frustration. It worked like a charm always. Mrs. Bernstein began.

JUST DREAM

When you're feeling sad
When something has you feeling mad
Don't give up…just dream.
Dream of what you would like to be
Dream of seagulls high above the sea.

When things don't go right
When someone's hurt you just for spite
Don't give up…just dream.
Dream of what you would like to be
Dream of doves soaring over the lea.

When you're tempted to be rude
To answer someone who's been wicked or crude
Don't give up…just dream.
Dream of how special you are to me
Dream of yourself as a bird in a tree.

Mrs. Bernstein finished reading. She folded the sheet, put it back in its envelope and returned it to her purse.

"That poem helped me a lot too" she said, without looking up. "It was so inspiring!" Then she reached over and grabbed Jessica's hand again. "Thank you Jessica…thanks for this gift." Jessica looked into her eyes.

"You're very welcome," she said softly.

They ate in silence for a while. Jessica broke the silence by inquiring again about the kids. Gradually the story came out. Mr. Bernstein had custodial rights over the children. Mrs. Bernstein was deeply hurt by this. They were only permitted to visit their mother on weekends. The children hardly ever saw their father (*what's new?*) and did not like the new nanny. They spoke of Jessica constantly. As for her mother-in-law, Mrs. Bernstein didn't care if she never saw her again. She was an interfering old goat. She will soon find out that no other daughter-in-law was going to be as kind to her as she (Mrs. Bernstein) was. She who allowed her to visit for two weeks every year and throw her a spectacular party as well. Jessica wondered about 'the butcher'. She was curious as to what part he played in this break-up.

"Are you living alone now?" Jessica asked. Mrs. Bernstein reddened with embarrassment.

"Yes," she answered, looking away from Jessica.

Before they left the restaurant, Jessica took out her now famous pink stationery from her briefcase and wrote a little note to Bernie and April. She signed it 'your friend, Jessica.' Mrs. Bernstein was elated. "They'll be so happy to hear from you," she said. Jessica watched as Mrs. Bernstein walked towards the parking lot - this woman, that many people would have said, had it all. The wind blew her hair in all directions. Her shoulders seemed to droop. The thick fox fur that she wore against the bitter cold, seemed only to emphasize the puniness that it sheltered.

****

Since Jessica was off work the following day as well, she met Willie at Carleton university and accompanied him to the auditorium in one of the buildings.

"What's going on there?" she asked. She didn't know where Willie was taking her and quite frankly she had some work to do. She had planned to spend her time at the library.

"A television program is filming a segment here," he said. "Let's go see what's it about."

"Who's the guest speaker?" she asked.

"It's some professor from another university," Willie answered. "He's a Nobel prize winner."

"Oh?"

"Yes," said Willie. "Apparently he has a theory that black people are genetically inferior to whites." Jessica steupsed loudly.

"Is this what you want me to waste my time with?" she asked Willie irritably. She knew all about those genetically superior people. Didn't she just have lunch with one of them yesterday? Did she not meet them on a daily basis since coming to this country? Whoever wanted to believe that…let them. Why was Willie wasting her time with this nonsense?

"Oh come and just listen for a while," Willie coaxed her, and just at that time they arrived at the auditorium door.

They sat towards the back of the packed auditorium and listened to what she felt was a barrage of insults and put downs, directed at black people, from this guest speaker. His remarks were interspersed with ardent clapping from the student body. He had conducted his questionable research in low income areas in London, England, it seemed. But the fact that he had been awarded the Nobel prize, albeit in physics, appeared to give credence to his racist views. Jessica was furious. She did not stay until the show ended.

"I've got to get some air," she said to Willie as she stepped over his legs on her way out.

She hurried over to the library where she found a quiet booth at the far corner, nearest the window. It was snowing lightly now. Yesterday, Mrs. Bernstein said her poem *Just Dream* had helped her. Jessica repeated the words to herself at the same time as her eyes followed the V formation of a bunch of Canada geese in the sky. She remembered when Aunt Mattie had advised her to stand tall and she thought of her grandmother - so regal and elegant. Determined not to allow the nonsense she'd heard in the auditorium to get her down, Jessica lifted two of her fingers in a V salute to her own reflection in the darkened window.

****

Flo and Chester returned from a holiday in Grenada. They phoned to talk about the trip when Jessica was visiting Madge and Willie. She picked up the extension in the bedroom and squatted yoga style on the carpeted floor. They had a great time with Flo's parents in Rockville and with Chester's family in Grandville.

But the political situation in the island was grim. Julian, who now had his 'papers' to come to Canada, was becoming involved in an anti-Gairy movement. There were several reports of violence between Gairy's supporters and opponents. Rumour had it, Flo said, that Shark was in a gang that supported Gairy. Both Daddy and Mammie were anxious for Julian to get away. They couldn't wait for him to leave Grenada.

Flo and Chester visited Ma Hilly on the hill. "She was her usual jolly self" Flo said. "They have a big, bad dog up there now. Josh and Jolene had to tie it up, so me and Chester could go up the hill."

" The children are absolutely beautiful and so smart" said Chester.

"They're both doing very well at school" continued Flo. "But we didn't see Aunt Mattie or Shark."

Everybody wanted to know why neither Flo nor Madge had any children yet. Did they not have Bailey blood in them? Their sister Lisa in Trinidad, was now a grandmother of three and Terri was close behind with two. Jessica could hear Madge wince. She had suffered at least three miscarriages and this was a very painful topic for her.

After graduating from Carleton, Willie got a diploma in education and had a teaching position in one of the area high schools. Now that Willie was settled, Madge confided in Jessica, she was going to take time off from her job at the bank at the very next pregnancy. She was determined not to lose another baby.

Fleurina, on the other hand, was frustrated with a regime of temperature taking "and all that crap" to pinpoint her fertile period. "I always thought getting pregnant was the easiest thing in the world," she said half jokingly to Jessica, " but now I know it can be damn hard." She and Chester had decided to quit the process prescribed by their fertility doctor and let the chips fall where they may. "This baby making business was taking all the romance out of our love making" she declared with a little smirk. Then added "If it's to be, it'll be."

****

Jessica and Curt spent a lot of time together. Sometimes she met him in Montreal - other times he came to Ottawa. They listened to a variety of different types of music. Curt was a real jazz enthusiast. They went to the movies and attended football games together. Frequently, they spent evenings at Madge and Willie's apartment. Curt was nothing like Jack. While one wouldn't put him in the 'handsome' category that Jack used to dominate, there was a quiet attractiveness about him. He was sensitive and caring. It was calming just being in his company. Jessica felt she could be her true self with him. She didn't feel the need to perform any 'out-of-body' role.

He was definitely not a dresser as Jack was in his heyday but he was humorous about it. When, with his permission, Jessica went through his wardrobe and took out several bags of clothes to be discarded, she witnessed the alarm on Curt's face.

"You're not throwing out these good pants...are you?"

"Say goodbye to Mr. Bellbottoms here," Jessica remarked laughingly.

"But there's nothing wrong with these pants...why are you throwing them out?" Curt asked again.

"The style has changed," Jessica responded.

"No it hasn't."

"Trust me Curt," added Jessica pointedly. *"Many years ago."* They both burst out laughing as Jessica tossed several pairs of outdated pants into a bag 'to go'.

The shopping expeditions that took place afterwards were enjoyable to both of them. Curt had to admit, even to himself, he looked fine in his new garb.

He relished the admiration in Jessica's eyes too, when he came out of the fitting room to model them.

"Feathers can definitely make the bird," she said as she gave him an admiring glance, whistling softly. Previously when Curt shopped, he put importance on the quality of the item rather than on its appearance or fit. Now Jessica had changed all that. She combined quality with appearance, fit and yes - cost.

Occasionally at work, someone he'd known for years, didn't recognize him or commented on how well he looked. There's something different about Curtis Lincoln now, many people remarked.

Often Jessica and Curt took long car rides together; both sharing the driving. They visited Niagara Falls and the Hamilton zoo. At Wonderland, they rediscovered the kids in themselves. They spent a weekend with Fleurina and Chester in Toronto. Despite rain showers, they joined the jump-up in the Caribana parade. Curt brought Jessica to meet his mother's family in Nova Scotia. There was a lot of laughter, fun and warmth when they were together.

Coming back from Toronto late one night, Jessica saw a different side to Curtis just as he also saw a new side to her. They were approaching a gas station.

"Do you need gas?" she asked him.
Curt shook his head and sped past the gas station. Jessica released the passenger seat to make herself more comfortable in a half lying position. She was dozing off when she felt the car sputtering. She sat up bewildered. She could see the lights of the next exit in the distance.

"What's the matter?" she asked. The car was limping off the highway onto the shoulder. It finally stopped.

"I think I'm out of gas" he said, not looking directly at Jessica.

"Out of gas?" Jessica didn't understand what was going on. She checked her watch. "But we just passed a gas station less than half an hour ago."

"Yes" said Curt, looking away from Jessica, sheepishly. "But I wanted to make it to the next station, which is not too far from here."

"Why?" *Am I missing something?*

"The next station gives points you can cash in," he confessed.

Jessica was furious. At three o' clock in the morning, there she was sitting alone on the highway, while Curt walked to the next gas station and luckily was able to 'thumb a ride' back to the car with a can of gas, all because he wanted some damned points. He learned that night what it felt like to make Jessica angry.

But sometimes Curt was as solid as a rock. She could rely on his good judgment. She spoke candidly to him of her children. She told him of her fear of being deported, like some women were, if she applied to bring up her children. That form she had filled out many years ago, stating she had no children, haunted her day and night. Curtis agreed with Madge and Willie that she should obtain Canadian citizenship first, before even attempting to apply for them.

So at exactly five years to the day that Jessica came to Canada, she applied for citizenship. She had almost completed a science degree at Carleton university, having switched to full time status in the past year. This involved some wheeling and dealing at work, which wasn't too difficult since she volunteered to work the 'graveyard' shifts - the least preferred of all shifts. It resulted in Jessica working full time and simultaneously being a full time student.

Very casually, one Saturday evening as they were walking in Vincent Massey park, Curtis suggested to Jessica that they move in together.

"Whaat?" Jessica wasn't sure she'd heard right. Curt was comfortable in Montreal and she had grown very fond of Ottawa, with its beautiful parks and gardens. The Rideau river which flowed through down town Ottawa added to the enchantment of this city. She didn't want to move.

"Yes…I think we should get married and move in together," Curt said again. Jessica remained silent. She moved closer to him to allow some joggers to pass by. *Is this a marriage proposal?*

"You know I'm bringing up the kids as soon as I get citizenship…right?"

"Of course I know that."

"So you want to marry a woman with two children?" Although Jessica enjoyed the relationship with Curt, she never expected it would become permanent. Somehow she thought that as soon as her children came, he'd simply take up his bed and walk. And she didn't blame him. Who wants to be saddled with a woman and another man's children. But he was a good man with a good heart and until that time she was going to enjoy his company.

"I love you Jessica and I want to become a permanent part of your life." They reached the incline of the hill and he stopped walking, held her hands in his and looked into her eyes as he spoke. She felt goose bumps all over her skin.

"You didn't answer my question," she said softly.

"I want to marry you even if you come with two children, a grandmother, a dog, a one legged cat, a bad temper sometimes, and very bossy all the time..." He said playfully and started running down the hill, expecting Jessica to follow him.

"Bad temper yourself," she shouted and began to pursue him.

"Then so be it...I still want to marry you," he finished up as Jessica approached him. At the bottom of the hill she caught up with him as he turned around. She ran straight into his open arms. He held her to his chest. She slipped her arms around his neck.

"Is this a yes?" he asked, whispering into her ear as he held her tightly.

"Yes...this is a yes" Jessica replied, burying her face in his neck. She was sure this was what she longed for - someone kind, caring, dependable and honest.

Madge and Willie came over that night with some bubbly to celebrate the engagement.

"I've got to tell you, Curt" Willie said, sipping his champagne. "I've had this bottle chilling ...waiting on this occasion for three years now."
Curtis smiled.

"So you're saying it's properly aged then," he retorted. They all laughed.

"Yes...Mr. Slow but Sure," said Madge.

"I was scared the darn thing would start to ferment," said Willie.

"I knew Jessica was the woman I'd been waiting for, since that day of the pretrial in Montreal...when we went out to dinner together," Curt said.

"Since then?"

"Yes...but there were ethical considerations. I just had to do my job and not mix anything else with it." Jessica recalled that day. It was on that day she'd discovered Curt's keen intelligence, wit, and the power of his smile which just warmed her all over.

"So where will you guys live...here in Ottawa or Montreal?" Madge asked.

"We haven't discussed that yet," answered Jessica

"I'm going to write the Ontario bar exams...just in case," said Curt.

CHAPTER 20

This past year had been difficult for Grandma. She could have sworn she had enough strength to hold it together for a long, long time. Lord knows she was trying hard but her health was failing. Last Sunday in church, some 'bad feelings' took hold of her. Luckily she always carried her vial of smelling salts in her purse. It was Jolene who fetched it out and held it to Grandma's nose. Then both Jolene and Ethel Bailey had to fan her until she felt better. Ethel said it was the heat in the church that caused these 'bad feelings' but Grandma didn't think so. Poor Mattie was no better. She was as haggard as a god horse these days. That arthritis was getting the better of her. No one could expect her to work in the land and pound cocoa and corn anymore.

The household was being supported mainly by what Jessica sent them from Canada. Grandma knew it couldn't be easy for her either but she had to hurry up and send for the children. Two old people just couldn't give them what they needed. Then with all the anti-government demonstrations and shootings taking place, she wanted those children far away from here. Ethel Bailey finally succeeded in getting Julian to go and join his sisters in Canada. He left last Sunday for Toronto. He was staying with Flo and her husband.

That Shark had been sounding off recently about wanting to have the back room to himself. He wanted his mother out of there. She could share the big room with Josh and Jolene, he said. He had some nerve. Grandma had to step in and tell him clearly that that room was for Mattie and if anybody had to move out, it was him. He was a big man now and could look after himself. The day Julian came up the hill to say goodbye, Grandma overheard Shark telling Julian, who had asked him why he didn't try to go abroad,

"You know boy...I wish I could a' go 'way like you, but me mother and auntie need me bad, man. If wasn't for dem...I gone long time...but dey need someone here to fen' for dem...you know...an' I got to do it." Grandma could hardly believe her ears. They needed Shark like they needed a cockroach in a pot of peas soup. They would be so much better off without him. For one thing the man ate like a damn barracuda...that name Shark suited him perfectly.

But there was a bigger problem with Shark recently. Josh and Jo were now eleven years old. They both used to be excellent students, but recently Josh was slackening off. The teachers complained that many times he didn't do his homework. He loved playing soccer and whenever he didn't do his homework Grandma wouldn't let him go near the soccer field. He didn't see why he had to do homework, he said. He asked Grandma why he couldn't stay home during the day like Uncle Shark. Like it or not, Shark's bad habits were influencing the children.

****

Jessica graduated from Carleton university with a science degree then obtained registration as a medical laboratory technologist. Curtis had written the Ontario bar exams and was now officially able to practice law in that province. As soon as her citizenship papers came through, Jessica wanted to apply for Josh and Jo to come to Canada but Curtis wanted her to wait until they were married before making application for the children. She couldn't believe that so many years had passed already. *My Gosh! Where did the time go?*

"Then there'll be no possible way they could even think of deporting you," he said and that made sense. The only problem was Jessica could see another delay - Curt also wanted them to sell their condominium apartments and buy a house together with room for the children before they even got here. That made sense too but the letters she received from Jolene and Grandma that day made Jessica determined to wait no longer.

"I'm going to apply for Josh and Jo to come to Canada," she said to Curtis over the phone that evening. Curtis was silent. He had just arrived at his apartment after a tiring day, when the phone rang. He was still in his coat. "So...can we get married this week then?"

"Jessica...what's the matter...what's the sudden rush about?"

"There's a big rush Curt," Jessica replied. He could hear the tremor in her voice. "I heard from Grandma and Jo today."

Grandma had written to tell Jessica how urgent it was for her to bring up the children *if you want to get them alive, that is*. She could sense her grandmother's impatience with her. Jessica felt guilty. For eight years she left the care of her children up to her grandmother. It was a shame and she wasn't going to wait any longer. What alarmed her though was what her grandmother went on to say in the rest of the letter. She found Josh playing with a gun that he found in the back room. It belonged to Shark. *He could have kill hisself, Jolene and all of us with the damn thing.* Jessica remembered the rumour that Shark was a member of a notorious gang. Yes, Grandma was right to be agitated and Jessica knew she had to do something about the situation now. *It too much for me*, Grandma's letter concluded, *and you have to take over now.* That was crystal clear.

Jolene's letter was far more disturbing. She stated that the teacher in school had beaten Joshua very badly for not doing his homework. Jo had allowed him to copy the homework from her, and although he had the correct answers, when the teacher asked him to do the sums on the board, he didn't have a clue what to do. *Mr. O'Reilly got out his biggest strap, which he calls Subjugator #3 and beat Josh until he peed himself in the class.* Jessica wept as she read this the first time and the tears flowed again when she reread it over the phone to Curt. Josh didn't want her to say anything about the incident to Grandma, so she was writing to tell her mother instead.

She said that Josh was acting like a real 'bad-john' recently. He told her that he was going to shoot that damn Mr. O'Reilly and all his subjugators. *I didn't believe him Mum, but the next day Grandma found Josh with Uncle Shark's gun.* Jessica was mortified. *I can stay here with Grandma and Aunt Mattie but Mum, please hurry up and send for Josh.* She felt the urgency in Jo's letter. For Jo to even suggest that they be separated, indicated to Jessica just how serious she felt the situation was.

What also triggered Jessica's attention was Jolene's requests from her mother. *Please send me a pair of spandex* shorts and size 32A bras. Bras? Jessica hadn't thought of it but her little girl was growing up. Neither did she realize that the 'little girl' dresses, she'd been sending until now, were definitely *passé*. In the pit of her stomach, she felt an urgency like never before. *God, if there is ever a time a girl needs her mother, it's now.* Although she'd been very busy, she had allowed herself to enter into that zone of tranquillity, relishing time spent with Curt, perhaps to the detriment of pressing responsibilities. With or without Curt, she was going to apply to bring the children up. Let the chips fall where they may.

Curtis came to Ottawa the next day and he and Jessica applied for a marriage license. They were married in a civil ceremony the following week with Willie and Madge as witnesses. They had dinner at a down town restaurant afterwards, but before that Jessica, now Mrs. Curtis Lincoln, submitted the application to bring Joshua and Jolene to Canada.

"I can't believe it," said Madge to Willie later that night. "Mr. Slowcoach actually got himself married with one week's notice."

"One week?" asked Willie. "It's been more like six or seven years."

"He didn't have the time to dot all the I's and cross all the T's."

"Now he has to move to Ottawa...I wonder how long that will take him."

****

Grandma made the happy announcement to friends and neighbours alike that Jessica had gotten married to a lawyer in Canada. Before they asked, she informed them that Jessica had started the 'papers' for Josh and Jo to go to Canada.

"So dey soon gwine be leavin' here," she said happily.

She passed by Mr. Farrow's store in town with the good news. She hadn't been there in years and it looked quite poorly. Albertine smiled at Grandma. She seemed to have lost a whole lot of weight. She wasn't the same stuck up pig she used to be. Mr. Farrow was glad to see Grandma and offered her a chair and a soft drink. Yes, Jessica had written to tell them of her marriage, he said. That Jessica was quite the lady. She got her BSc and a diploma in something else too. Grandma nodded in agreement - she was quite the woman.

The children were doing fine. Debbie was working in Barbados now. Trevor still had one more year in high school before writing his graduation exams. They corresponded with Jessica from time to time. One Sunday soon, he and Trevor were going to come up the hill to take the twins to the beach. Grandma was welcome to come along but only if she wore her bikini. Ha! Ha! Did they still have the bad dog? Grandma told him that Spice was still there but was an old woman just like she was.

"Like you?...Then she's got a whole lot of bite in her still," Ian assured Grandma with a mischievous grin across his face.

Albertine offered up the news that Jack DeCoutreau had returned to the island.

"Oh yes?"

"He came for his father's funeral" said Ian, "and he hasn't gone back yet. I don't know if he's going back at all."

"I hear he walk out on his wife an' four children."

"Oh well…" said Grandma. Jack wasn't a topic she was particularly interested in. She didn't even think of the twins as being half DeCoutreau. For their entire life not a single one in that family had acknowledged them.

"You not gwine believe how bad he lookin'," said Albertine. Grandma got a glimpse of Albertine, the old gossip monger, still there.

"You mus' be jokin'," said Grandma.

"An' he drinkin' worse dan any sailor." Grandma shook her head as she mused to herself. So this is what he had come to - the athletic, handsome Jack DeCoutreau, who treated Jessica like a piece of crap - she wasn't good enough for him. Grandma snorted. If you wait long enough, it all just comes right around.

****

Curt and Jessica visited some model homes in the west end of Ottawa. The homes were spacious and elegant. They had heard of this new development from Madge and Willie, who had already purchased a home in that area. They were scheduled to take possession of it in about six months, as soon as the construction was completed.

"It would be so nice if we could be neighbours," Madge said excitedly.

"Location is the most important thing, when it comes to buying a house," Willie said. He spoke of the beautiful parks with recreational facilities nearby and the good schools within walking distance. He taught in one of them himself. Jessica could see many advantages but the disadvantage was that any home they purchased now in this development, wouldn't be ready for a whole year. She couldn't wait that long for her children to join her.

They eventually settled on a split level, also in the west end of Ottawa. It was less than ten minutes drive from Madge and Willie's new home. A real estate agent told them of this property that was very reasonably priced. The previous occupants were moving out to Vancouver and were anxious to sell quickly. After ensuring that all the construction checks and cost of the house were to their satisfaction, Curt and Jessica signed on the dotted line. Two months later they moved into this house.

Jessica was happy as there was more than sufficient space for the children. The back yard had a large deck, one side of which led to the gate of a fenced-in section which separated an in-ground pool from the rest of the back yard.

"It's beautiful here" said Curt, and Jessica agreed. She pictured Josh and Jo splashing about and enjoying this pool.

Jessica set about furnishing the children's bedrooms right away. She was excited that finally they would have separate rooms to themselves. She couldn't wait to see their faces. While she knew that material trappings could not in any way replace the years in their lives she had missed, she nevertheless hoped these comforts would help to ease the transition from their beloved home to life in a new country.

Yet feelings of guilt bothered Jessica. It helped to recall that both Grandma and her father had sanctioned her move to Canada, so that she could make a better life for herself and her children. No one imagined that so many years would have elapsed before they could be reunited. But these guilty feelings persisted and to quell them Jessica worked doubly hard preparing for her children's arrival.

It seemed to Curt that Jessica was thoroughly consumed with getting everything ready for the children. Sometimes he would lie awake late at night wondering whether or not he was losing his foothold from that lofty position he once occupied in her life.

CHAPTER 21

Thirteen year old Joshua and Jolene finally arrived in Canada, nine years after their mother had done so. Curt and Jessica as well as Fleurina, Chester and Julian were at the airport in Toronto to meet them. Joshua was just like he appeared in his pictures - tall, slim, dark and so handsome. Jolene surprised Jessica even more. At thirteen, she had blossomed into an attractive and physically well developed young woman. She could easily have passed for sixteen.

Jessica spotted them as soon as they entered the waiting area.

"There they are," she said to Curt as she rushed forward to embrace them. She and Curt had been waiting for over an hour at the airport. Even though the flight was due at seven p.m., Jessica insisted they get to the airport for at least six thirty. She remembered that cold, dismal night she arrived in Montreal without a soul at the airport to meet her. She remembered how lost she felt. No way on earth her children were going to have that experience too. Fleurina and the others arrived much later but still well before the children cleared customs and came out into the waiting area.

"Hi Mum!" Joshua smiled shyly, as though greeting a stranger, when Jessica embraced him. Jolene returned her mother's hug but noticing they were blocking the path of other passengers, Jessica released her daughter. Curt came forward to take the luggage cart that Jolene was pushing.

"This is Uncle Curt," said Jessica, introducing Curt as she walked arm in arm with her son and daughter to the area where Chester, Flo and Julian were standing. When they were finally in a less crowded spot, everyone hugged and welcomed the newcomers and inquired of the trip. Curt hugged them both adding a kiss for Jolene.

"I can hardly believe you guys are finally here," said Jessica, drying her eyes. It was such an emotional moment for her. She felt weak with happiness but deep down there was a little bit of sadness when she looked at her children. She had missed out on a big chunk of their lives; a part that could never ever be replaced.

They spent the night in Toronto with Flo and Chester and early the next morning, after breakfast, drove to Ottawa. Jessica was anxious for the children to be in their new home. She promised Julian that before the end of the summer they would return for him to show them around Toronto.

"When we gwine reach?" ask Josh as they traveled East on the trans-Canada highway. It seemed like he'd been traveling forever. They passed miles and miles of corn - just corn. Then it seemed there were miles upon miles of just hay. He never realized this place was so huge.

"In another hour," answered Jessica.

"So long?" he asked.

Curt said nothing but noted it was the third time Joshua had asked that same question.

"Pass my bag," Jolene said to Josh. The next instant, Jessica heard the rustle of a wrapper being removed from a chocolate bar. She was about to tell them to be careful not to spill any bits in the car. Curt was most meticulous and particular about his *Volvo*. She said instead,

"We'll soon be home guys…you don't want to spoil your lunch…right?"

At about twelve thirty, they pulled into their driveway. Jessica unlocked the front door, while Curt took the bags out of the trunk. The children cautiously entered their new home.

"Come let me show you your bedrooms," said Jessica slipping off her shoes and leading the way up the carpeted stairs. She turned left at the top of the landing. A small wicker table with two chairs framed an elegant bay window at the opposite end from the landing. Through this port, the brilliance of the sun softly welcomed the newcomers as Jessica pointed out their spacious new bedrooms.

"This one is your room, Josh" she opened the door to the first room. It sported blue drapes and matching bed spread that Jessica had made herself.

"Nice," said Josh as he and Jolene entered to admire the room.

"This one over here is yours, Jo" Jessica said to Jolene. The second room was slightly more fancy. The furniture was all white contrasting with the green and pink pattern of the drapes and spread. On the dressing table were two framed photographs of the twins when they were much younger. Jolene's eyes noticeably widened in surprise as they roamed over the room, but her verbal response was,

"It's okay." A lukewarm response that jolted Jessica a bit. She had gone to great lengths to make the rooms as comfortable as possible. But she was aware that no amount of material trappings could replace the time she had been absent from their lives.

"And this is your bathroom here," she continued. It opened from a door in the hallway between the two bedrooms.

"And what's in here?" Joshua was opening another door next to the bathroom in the hallway. He seemed a lot more spontaneous and relaxed than Jolene.

"That's the linen closet," answered Jessica, as they both peered inside.

"Here are your bags" said Curt, coming upstairs with their bags which he deposited in the hallway before returning downstairs.

"Where's your bedroom, Mum?" asked Josh.

"In here," said Jessica and led the way to the door on the right side of the stairs. The room was huge and they admired the teak furniture. They saw blown up pictures of themselves and Grandma on the walls.

"Wo-o-oy!" There's another bathroom here," said Josh. He was evidently impressed. "And Jo" he called to his sister. "Come see this room here…just for clothes."

"And where his room?" Jolene asked Jessica before following Josh into the large walk-in closet. She gestured with her chin to someone outside the bedroom; obviously referring to Curt.

"Uncle Curt?" Jessica asked and Jolene nodded. Jessica noticed that neither of the children had yet referred to Curt, as 'Uncle Curt'. She was beginning to suspect that this was intentional.

"This is Uncle Curt's room too," she said wondering at the strangeness of the question. Then feeling the need to underline Curt's position in the household, went on to say very deliberately "This house belongs both to Uncle Curt and me. He is your new Daddy."

"I don't need no Daddy," Jolene mumbled defiantly. Jessica sensed some resentment or was it hurt in her daughter's tone. She couldn't quite put her finger on it at the moment. Instead, she put her arm around her daughter's shoulders, as Josh rushed past them downstairs.

"I want to see the rest of the house," he said. "Come on Jo." They all went downstairs. The dinette table was already set for lunch. They looked at the unfinished basement and then went to the backyard. While Jessica had been working hard preparing the inside of the house, Curt had been working just as hard in the backyard, ever since they moved into the property. He stained the fence and deck and planted shrubs and bushes, some of which had already begun to bloom. What fascinated the children most was when Curt opened the gate to reveal the grand in-ground swimming pool. It took their breath away.

"Nice!" said Josh.

"We can swim here whenever we want to?" asked Jolene.

"Almost...but Uncle Curt will tell you the rules," said Jessica relieved that Jo was finally becoming animated.

After the children were washed up and changed they had lunch together at the dinette table.

"We'll phone Grandma right after lunch," said Jessica. Before they ate, they all joined hands and thanked God for this day. Jolene noticeably tried to take the seat between Josh and her mother, but Jessica was firm.

"No...this is my seat, Jo" she said. So Jolene had to take the seat on her left and Josh sat to her right. Each of the children had to hold hands with her and with Curt as they bowed heads and prayed together. Like it or not, Curt was a part of this family and they had to get used to him.

During lunch Jessica discovered that she had a lot of work to do, regarding the children's table manners. Josh ate quickly and noisily. Jolene licked her fingers. They didn't seem to know how to use a knife and fork properly. Jessica could feel Curt's eyes on her, expecting her to correct the children. *Not today. Not at our very first meal together as a family.* She remembered Grandma used to be very meticulous about table manners when she was a little girl. *Whatever happened?* Jessica immediately felt ashamed of that thought. How could she possibly expect her poor grandmother - now almost eighty years old - to have the strength to raise her two children as fastidiously as she raised her. When Josh burped loudly at the table, that was the last straw for Curt. He pushed back his chair and with a loud 'excuse me' left the room.

"What's wrong with him?" asked Jolene, inclining her chin towards the door that had just closed behind Curt.

"Nothing's wrong with Uncle Curt," replied Jessica softly. She was feeling annoyed with Curt for being so thin skinned as much as she was frustrated at Jolene's determination to refer to Curt as 'him'. "But guys from tomorrow, we're going to learn some table manners around here. Okay?" she smiled at both of them. They looked at her curiously then at each other.

"Anybody for dessert?" asked Jessica, when they had finished the main course. Before leaving for Toronto yesterday, she had made and iced a heart-shaped cherry cake, on which she wrote "Joshua & Jolene Welcome Home." Even though part of her wanted to ignore him, she decided to invite Curt to share their dessert. She went to the garage where he was tending to his car.

"Dessert is being served Curt... coming?"

"Did you see the mess they made behind here?" he asked referring to chocolate bits that were spilled and crushed in the back seat and floor of the car. *God guide me, please.*

"Curt...the children have only just arrived. I know I have a big and difficult job ahead of me. I only hope you'll be by my side to help and support me." *And not make this a helluva lot more difficult as you're doing right now.*

"But you're not even bothering to correct them."

"I will...starting tomorrow. Today...let's just chill." Then going to him and putting an arm around his waist, she asked again with a smile,

"Coming for dessert?"

Inside the children were excitedly examining the cake.

"I want that piece with my name," Jo was saying, but they stopped talking as soon as Jessica and Curt entered the room. Jessica cut and served the cake.

"So...do you know how to bake?" Jessica asked them, trying to break the silence, which was helping to emphasize the smacking sounds coming from Joshua's mouth.

"Yes" said Jo, with a big piece of cake threatening to fall from her mouth. She swooped it back in with her middle finger. "I know how to make Christmas cake and sponge cake."

"And coconut bun," said Josh.

"You don't know how," said Jolene. "I can bake but Josh don't know how."

"Okay," said Jessica. "We'll just have to teach him then."

"That's for girls," mumbled Josh.

"If you like eating it…it's not a bad idea to learn how to make it too" said Curt, trying to participate in the conversation. Neither of the children responded. *My job's not going to be easy.*

Nine critical years had passed since Jessica was physically in the role of mother. She knew the road ahead was going to be bumpy - at the very least. These children were as unfamiliar to her as she was to them. Not to mention Curt - a brand new father that she was now introducing into their lives. Her heart was heavy as she silently begged God for strength and patience.

****

The house felt empty when Grandma returned from the airport. Mr. Farrow had driven them all to the airport, early that morning. Thank God, Mrs. Gittens's daughter, whom Jessica used to give lessons to, was also going to Barbados. She promised Grandma that she would look out for Josh and Jo - make sure they switched to the right plane in Barbados, for Toronto.

She went to her bed early that evening. She didn't feel like eating a thing. She still slept in a curtained off part of the living room. The next day she was going to move back into the big bedroom that the twins had vacated. Jessica had encouraged her to add another bedroom to the house, but Grandma strongly refused. She accepted the repairs and painting to the house, some new furniture, colour television set, telephone and lots of other improvements but not an extra bedroom. That would simply encourage Shark to stay forever, she thought.

"Drink dis hot cup a' cocoa tea," Aunt Mattie was saying to Grandma.
She noticed Grandma hadn't eaten anything the evening before when she came back from the airport. She knew that losing the twins was hitting her hard, even though she'd been waiting nine years for Jessica to send for them. The house felt like a graveyard without the twins. She could tell from the way Hilda dragged her feet coming up the hill and turned in to bed right away, that she was taking it very hard. She didn't even watch TV from the verandah, with the neighbours who dropped by.

"Thanks Mattie…rest it on de table for me, please," answered Grandma. When Aunt Mattie checked on her an hour later, the cocoa tea was untouched and cold; a white rim of fat settling at the top. She took it away, returning a while later with some hot chicken soup for her sister.

"I make you some chicken soup dis time an' I not gwine leave till you drink it."
Grandma sat up in bed, her head swooning. She felt weak. She shakily took the bowl from Aunt Mattie, who sat beside her on the bed to help her and make sure she didn't spill the hot liquid on herself. She felt better once she had drunk it.

"What time it is, Mattie?" The clock on the table was saying two o' clock but that had to be wrong. Just then the phone rang. Aunt Mattie answered it.

"Hello."

"Aunt Mattie…how are you? It's Jessie."

"Jessie Doux Doux? What's up…Darlin'? De children wid you?"

It was Jessica calling from Canada. The children must have arrived safely. Praise to God, thought Grandma. She heard Mattie talking to each of the children, before she handed her the phone.

"Grandma…this is Jolene…how yoh feelin' today, Ma?"

"I'm doin' well Joly Darlin'" answered Grandma, and indeed she was suddenly feeling energized. "How y'all find de trip?"

"The trip was great Ma…the plane was delayed only forty five minutes in Barbados. You know Grandma…the plane was flying way above the clouds."

"Miss Gittens help you find de plane for Toronto?"

"It was easy, Ma. We found it easy." Jolene didn't feel like explaining to Grandma that in Barbados the incoming and outgoing passengers were separated. Beyond a certain point, they couldn't stay together.

"Thank God."

"Any bad feelings take you since we leave, Ma?" Jolene wanted to know. Grandma had been having frequent fainting spells recently and it worried Jolene.

"No Sweetheart…none…I feelin' good." Grandma didn't see the point of telling her that she'd remained weak in bed until a few minutes ago.

"Love you lots Grandma and Mum say we can talk to you every week."

"You write to me sometimes instead of makin' expensive phone calls," cautioned Grandma. Economizing was an instinct that came to her naturally.

"Yes Ma."

"How Uncle Curt?"

"Fine Ma...here's Josh now Ma...Bye Ma."

"Bye Sweetheart."

Josh took the phone.

"Hi Grandma."

"Hi Darlin'...how you like yoh new home?"

"You should see it, Ma...it nice for so...Jo and I have we own room now."

"Yes?...dat's great. Make sure you keep it tidy...okay?"

"Yes Ma."

"And Josh...remember to be a good boy...don' do anyt'ing wild...okay?"

"Yes Ma."

"And Josh..." But before Grandma could remind Josh of something else to do or not to do, Josh butted in,

"Ma...you move back to the big room yet?"

"Not yet...but today for sure," she answered.

"How Spice doin' Ma?"

"Fine Sweetheart." Truth was Grandma hadn't seen Spice since she came back home from the airport, but she was sure Mattie had taken care of her. Josh had been very attached to Spice and leaving her was one additional burden on him.

"Mum want the phone now Ma...but say hello to Spice and Jacob and Uncle Shark...okay?"

"Yes Darlin'."

"Love you Ma."

"Love you too, Sweetheart."

Jessica now had the phone. She told Grandma how surprised she was to see the children so grown. She said how handsome they both were. She thanked Grandma for the rum and other goodies she sent and inquired about her health. She promised that as soon as the children were settled, she was going to come home for a visit. Curt was eager to meet her and Aunt Mattie. He'd heard so much about them.

"That would be so nice, Jessie." Suddenly Grandma felt like a young woman again. "So so nice," she repeated.

"I can hardly wait, Ma."

"Give Curt a big hug and kiss for me...and Jess," Grandma paused for a brief moment then continued. "Be patient wid de children...it goin' to take time...but jus' be patient, Darlin'."

There went her grandmother again. How did Grandma know that Jessica already had to invoke the Almighty to grant her strength and patience in her new role?

Later that evening Madge and Willie came by to greet the children.

"I can't believe how nicely my godchildren growing," commented Madge, after she'd hugged and kissed them almost to death.

"Uncle Willie and I wanted to buy you a welcoming gift, but your Mum and Uncle Curt said to wait until you get here. So how about if we go together next Saturday to pick out something?"

Josh smiled broadly. Jolene's eyes lit up.

"Shopping? I love shopping," she exclaimed.

Madge and Jessica were sitting by the pool watching while Jo and Josh splashed and played around in the water. Once in a while her father used to take them to Grand Anse with Trevor, but this was not consistent. *They could use some formal lessons.* She decided to register them for swimming lessons this summer. Willie donned his swimming trunks and joined the children in the pool. Curt was cooking up some goodies at the barbecue.

"Do you like basketball?" Willie asked Josh.

"He only like soccer, Uncle Willie" answered Jolene. "He would never play tennis with me."

"Not true, Uncle Willie...I like all kind o' sport. I never play basketball though."

"In the park behind our home there are basketball hoops, badminton nets...you guys must come over and play..."

"There's lots to do" said Jessica. "We have to sit down and decide what you will choose."

Jessica noticed the ease with which the children slipped into 'Uncle Willie'. She was sure Curt had also picked up on it. We just have to be patient, she reminded herself, but she couldn't help that feeling of anxiety in the pit of her stomach.

CHAPTER 22

"Mattie," Grandma called out to her sister. "You have a letter here from England." Jacob came up the hill that evening with a bunch of letters.

"Looots of leeetters toooday. Maa Hiiily."

"Wo-o-o-y! Thanks Jacob" replied Grandma, feeling very proud and important. She scanned the envelopes. There was one from Jessica, with the usual money order. There was one each from Jolene and Josh. Both Jolene and Josh had written to herself and Aunt Mattie giving them all the details of their trip and their new home which had a backyard with a big swimming pool. Jo wrote that they went shopping twice - once with her mother, and another time with Auntie Madge, who lives not too far from them. *You have to see those huge shopping centers, Ma,* Jolene wrote. Grandma smiled. They seemed to be enjoying their new surroundings and she was happy but she didn't think she was going to see the new shopping centers. Her time for that had long passed.

But it was the fourth letter, addressed to *Mrs. Matilda Bennett* that had Grandma totally mystified. Who could be writing Mattie from England? It couldn't possibly be Dawson after all these years. It looked like an official type envelope. It was brown with a little window showing her old Gauvine address. The post office had rerouted it to Rockville. This person certainly wasn't current, whoever he or she was. Mattie had been living with her in Rockville for close to nineteen years now.

"Mattie!" she called again.

"What's up Hilda?"

"You have a letter here from England."

Aunt Mattie slowly came around from the back of the house, wiping her hands in her apron. She took a seat in the rocking chair. Grandma was sitting in one of the wicker chairs nearby. She didn't want to appear too eager, but she couldn't wait to find out what that letter was all about. Aunt Mattie slowly examined the envelope and tore it open. She read it silently - there seemed to be a few pages - and returned it to the envelope.

"Well?" asked Grandma. She could hold back her curiosity no longer. "Who it from?"

"It from de English government," said Aunt Mattie, as she passed the letter to Grandma. "Here…read it nuh."

The letter was not from Dawson but it was about Dawson; the husband who Mattie had not heard from for over twenty five years. Due to complications from diabetes, he was now blind and recently had one of his legs amputated. The British government wanted to send him home to his wife and family, which was apparently Mr. Bennett's desire. There was a form for his wife to fill out and return in the enclosed envelope. In disbelief Grandma looked over at her sister.

"Dey serious?" she asked.

"Dey could serious if dey want," answered Aunt Mattie, getting up stiffly from the rocking chair.

Aunt Mattie started going towards the back of the house, when she threw back her head in a fit of cheerless laughter. For a moment Grandma thought she was wailing. Aunt Mattie was surprised at how free she felt. Something Jessica had said to her a long time ago came to mind. Something about not letting what other people do, eat away at you - giving them the power. "Let it go Auntie" Jessica had urged. Now she was sure she had done just that. The laughter that had begun in her throat now exploded up from her chest and belly. Grandma couldn't contain her own deep laughter either. Spice, who spent most of her time sleeping on a cushion underneath the house, awoke to add her feeble yelps as well.

Ethel Bailey, starching clothes at a concrete sink in her back yard down below, stopped to listen to the unaccustomed chorus from above. What on earth was going on up there, she wondered. A few hours later as she was about to hang out the coloured clothes, she turned around to see Mattie coming towards her. What did that scarecrow woman want now?

"Hi Ethel," said Aunt Mattie with a smile. Surprised, Mrs. Bailey dropped the towel she was about to hang.

"Hi Mattie," she replied.
Aunt Mattie was carrying a dish with some cashews. "I pick up a whole lot o' cashew dat de wind blow down dis mornin'...you want some?"
Mrs. Bailey blinked. Was this Mattie Bennett being nice to her now - the first time in about forty years? Yet there was something genuine in Mattie's eyes.

"Sure," Mrs. Bailey smiled and accepted the gift. "How 'bout comin' in for some nice soursop juice dat I squeeze dis mornin'?"

"Sure," answered Aunt Mattie and they tottered into the kitchen.

Over the next few weeks neighbours dropping by the Bailey's home received the shock of their lives. They could hardly believe their eyes and ears. Ethel Bailey and Matilda Bennett were chatting and giggling like two old teenage friends.

****

Jessica registered both children for swimming lessons at the sportsplex. Even though it was past the registration period for summer soccer, Willie was able to get Josh into a team in the area. Not wanting Jo to feel left out, Jessica searched high and low for some place which offered tennis lessons. Finally, at much expense, she found a private tennis coach for Jolene. When Willie suggested that he give them some math and English lessons before they started school, Jessica jumped at the idea. She was worried that Josh might be behind in math. Willie's suggestion was perfect.

So their schedules were very busy. On Monday and Thursday mornings they took the bus over to the sportsplex for their swimming lessons. On Tuesday evenings, Josh walked over to his soccer practice in a nearby park, while Jessica had to hurry home to drive Jolene to and from her tennis lesson. The same routine took place on Wednesday but this time Jessica drove Josh to and from his soccer game. On Thursday evenings she brought them over to Madge and Willie's home for their academic lessons.

"I can never thank Willie enough for this," Jessica said to Madge as they sat together in the Johnson's backyard one Thursday. Willie had refused to take any payment from Jessica for tutoring the children.

"If the children do well in school...that will more than thank him," Madge replied. Jessica felt guilty that Willie and Madge did not yet know of her decision to register the children at St. Thomas's and not Forrest Stetson high school, where Willie taught.

"I'm going tomorrow to register them at St. Thomas's," Jessica said.

"Oh?" replied Madge, surprised.

"It's just ten minutes walk from home," went on Jessica.

"That's right," answered Madge. She knew Willie was going to be disappointed but St. Thomas's was supposed to be a good school too.

Curt was already home when they returned. Jessica felt herself thinking "Oh my goodness... I didn't have time to dash around the house fixing any messes the kids may have made before Curt came home."

"Hi Honey...how're you doing?" said Jessica leaning over to kiss him on the cheek. He was sitting at the kitchen table reading the paper, while having a plate of what looked like 'take out'.

"Hi," said Josh and Jo as they raced upstairs.

"Hi," Curt returned the greeting to all.

Jessica went to the refrigerator and took out some noodles that she had made for supper the day before.

"The children have already eaten," she said. "I thought the two of us would eat together tonight."

"Yes" said Curt, indicating with a gesture that he was almost finished eating. "And what a big mess someone made over on the counter there."

Jessica knew that Josh and Jo were not 'fine tuners' when it came to house work. They would often leave the kitchen sink dirty or the counters unwiped and Jessica would have to get them to return to finish their work. Today she was running late when she arrived from work and dashed out before checking the house.

"Is that right?"

"Yes and someone left the gate to the pool open again. I've told them a million times already to close the gate when they're done."

Jessica heated up her plate of mixed noodles, vegetables and chicken and sat beside Curt at the table.

"I'll be sure to tell them to shut the gate to the pool," she said softly. "Or else they wouldn't be allowed to use it."

"It's a matter of safety" said Curt, a little surprised at Jessica's soft but harsh reaction. He wondered whether she was mad at him for complaining.

Today she was planning to talk to Curt about getting bicycles for the children and she also wanted to get his approval regarding her choice of St. Thomas's high school. She wanted to ask him to come with them to Joshua's soccer game on Wednesday and some Tuesdays if he was able he could take Jolene to her tennis lesson. In other words she wanted him to become more involved in the children's lives. Instead he seemed to stand on the side lines and criticize them. Yes, they were not perfect. No children were. The job of a parent was to love and teach them. She felt as though she were in a tug-of-war, being pulled from two sides.

When Curt had arrived home earlier than usual that day, it was with the hope that they could all drive down to the bicycle shop to look at bicycles for the children. They would like this, he thought. He felt a disconnect with them which he hoped this would help.

They seemed to shy away from him. They didn't seem relaxed in his presence and this saddened him. For the first time this week he received an 'Uncle Curt' from Josh. It was yet to come from Jolene.

As the garage door opened he realized with regret that Jessica's *Camry* was not there. Oh no, he thought, they've gone some place. He felt a little peeved. He entered the house from the garage and approached the kitchen. The sink was filled with dirty dishes and on the counter was a huge mess. It looked like someone had spilled spaghetti sauce and didn't have the good sense to clean it up.

Curt was beginning to feel irritated. He placed his briefcase on the floor by the kitchen table, took a cold beer from the fridge and opened the back door which led onto the deck. The gate to the swimming pool area was gaping open. He definitely was mad at this point. He slammed the gate shut and bolted it.

"Over and over I've told them to keep this gate shut," he said to himself. He sat on the deck with tie loosened, for sometime - the beer in his hand half resting on the table next to him. When he did take a sip from the bottle, it had already lost its coldness. Curt went into the house. He dumped the lukewarm liquid down the sink. He missed Jessica. She hardly seemed to have time for him these days.

He wasn't quite sure where he was going as he got back into his car. The Chinese restaurant a few blocks down the road seemed to call his name. Realizing how starved he was, he pulled into the parking lot. He ordered 'take out' because he didn't feel like sitting in a restaurant. Perhaps he would drive over to one of the parks nearby and eat there, he thought, but looking down at himself still in his work clothes, he canceled that idea. He went back home. Before sitting down to eat, he cleaned up the messy kitchen. He retrieved the *Ottawa Citizen* from his briefcase and was in the middle of his meal when he heard Jessica arrive with the children.

Jessica finished her meal in silence, then she cleaned up carefully and meticulously - just like Curt. Before she left the kitchen she marinated some chicken to be cooked the next day. The children were still upstairs by the time she was done. She would go upstairs in a while to talk to them. She felt Curt encircling her with his arms from behind.

"Let's go have a dip in the pool, Love" he said, kissing the side of her neck.

"No" she answered, swinging around to face him. His arms dropped to his side. "I have to go blast the children for all the bad things they've been doing. Remember?" She knew this was a low blow but right then she just couldn't stop herself. Curt looked hurt - as though she had physically wounded him.

Jessica went upstairs but instead of knocking at the children's rooms, went to her own room and threw herself across the bed. She heard the stereo which Curt had given the children, playing in Josh's room. This job was much more difficult than she had anticipated, and it had only just begun. She told herself that Curt meant well and she had to be more patient with him. The children were already making great strides. They were happy most of the time. Jolene was a big help in preparing meals or finishing meals that Jessica had started. They both helped with the vacuuming and dusting. Willie told her their math and English were improving by leaps and bounds. Just yesterday she heard Josh refer to Curt as 'Uncle Curt'. Now that was a big step. She simply had to be constant and gentle in correcting their shortfalls. It was unrealistic for Curt to expect them to walk on water and she was going to tell him so.

She was contemplating returning downstairs to speak to Curt when she heard the door to the garage slam loudly. He was going out. She went to the window upstairs and saw Curt reversing his car down the driveway. Where is he going now, she wondered. Sadly she shook her head as the words of the song *Many Rivers to Cross* popped into her mind. She took a seat in one of the wicker chairs and picked up an *Essence* magazine.

As if the slamming of the garage door was a cue, the doors to both bedrooms opened and the children came out into the hallway.

"Let's go down to the bicycle shop," Jessica said to them. She hadn't mentioned anything about bicycles to them before and enjoyed seeing their eyes brighten.

"Why we lookin' at bicycles...we goin' to get bicycles?" Jolene asked. Jessica thought she'd be a little mysterious.

"That depends," she answered. "But in the meantime it doesn't hurt to look."

"What it depends on, Mum?" asked Josh.

"It depends on you both...how well you do your chores and clean up after yourselves...and remember to close the gate to the pool," answered Jessica.
The children shot knowing glances at each other. She knew they had been eavesdropping and heard Curt's complaints. Jessica continued as she looped an arm around each of them,

"So far you guys are doing very well..."

"Yes?"

"But I want you to try just a little bit harder..."

"We will Mum...I'll make sure the kitchen is spotless, even though I wasn't the one dirtying up," said Jo as she stuck her tongue out playfully at her brother.

"I'll make sure the gate to the pool is always shut," promised Josh and, to get back at Jo, he added "even though I wasn't the last one in the pool."

"And if you do...then it's bicycles...here we come," said Jessica loudly as she squeezed both children towards her.

After they got out of the car, Josh observed Curt's *Volvo* parked right beside them, in the parking lot of the bicycle store. They went into the store and sure enough there he was. The children were too thrilled by the thought of new bicycles to let his presence dim their excitement.

"Hi Honey," said Jessica going towards him. She wasn't going to carry resentment any longer. "What're you doing here?"
Curt was so surprised to see them that he blurted out excitedly,

"I can get a real good deal on bicycles for the children."

"Yes?" said Jessica putting an arm around his shoulders, while looking around to make sure the children did not hear this. They were busily examining a gold and black bicycle on display. "But shhh...they have to fulfill their part if they are to get bicycles." She was amazed and thrilled that she and Curt were thinking along the same lines. Curt smiled. He was relieved that Jessica was not still upset at him. All he wanted was what was best for her and the children. He put his arm around her waist and discreetly brushed his lips against her forehead.

On the way home after looking at and trying out many bicycles, they all stopped off for ice cream at *Creamy Cold*. They sat together on a picnic bench and licked away at their cones.

"You have to lick much faster than that," Josh said to Jolene, who had chocolate ice cream running down her arms. "Here let me help you." But Jolene moved her ice cream cone away before Josh could take a hearty lick from it.

"No way," she said. They all laughed. It was Curt who handed her a bunch of napkins to clean up her arm. *Maybe there is hope for this family, after all.* Jessica felt very grateful for the togetherness that she was witnessing between Curt and the children. She knew there would be ups and downs but prayed that they would keep going in the right direction.

At midnight, long after the children were asleep, Jessica came to Curt who had just finished watching the late news on TV.

"How about that dip in the pool now?" she asked.

"Whaaat?" he asked. She was wearing her robe and looked like she was about to go to bed but she was carrying beach towels in her arms.

"Yes" she said, slipping off the robe. She was buck naked underneath.

"With an offer like that..." Curt hastened out of his clothes and they chased each other into the pool.

CHAPTER 23

St. Thomas's high school was a sprawling gray stone building with soccer fields adjoining. Curt accompanied Jessica and the twins to the children's registration. Taking Jessica's suggestion, he was trying to become much more involved in their lives. Jessica brought along a copy of the curriculum and the children's last report cards from the Rockville school. While Joshua's final report was fair, thanks to a lot of prodding and persuasion from Grandma, Jolene had an outstanding record.

After filling out registration forms, they were shown into the tiny office of Mr. Gordon, the vice-principal of the school. It seemed that Josh's brilliance on the soccer field had preceded him.

"Joshua Farrow...I've heard of you," he said excitedly, adjusting his glasses to make sure he had indeed read the name correctly from the form before him, on the desk. Josh grinned. Jolene waited for some sort of recognition for herself.

"I hope you join our school's soccer team, Josh" the vice-principal continued. "Jeff Roman told me all about you. You're a fantastic soccer player." Jeff Roman, a teacher at St. Thomas's, happened to be one of the coaches on the soccer team Josh played for during the summer. Josh was visibly flattered. "Have you seen our soccer fields?" Josh nodded. Mr. Gordon's eyes flashed with exuberance as he described in detail how closely St. Thomas's soccer team got to the finals last semester. "We were this close" he said, holding up his thumb and forefinger almost touching each other.

Jessica tried to steer the conversation back to the academic curriculum. She knew that Jolene was beginning to feel left out.

"When do they do math?" she asked, trying to focus on the timetable she was given.

"I don't see any languages here either," said Curt, looking over Jessica's shoulder at the sheet she was holding.

"Oh no," said the vice principal, interrupting his soccer conversation with Josh. "Children in the B stream don't have to do math and languages."

Jessica's antennae were suddenly tuned in. Willie had warned her about this. I can't tell you the number of children who were doing very well in the schools back home, he said, but come up here and are channeled into the B stream.

"How many different streams are there?" Jessica asked softly.

"Two," answered the vice-principal. "The B stream is usually much more suitable for newcomers to Canada."

"And the A stream?"

"The children would find it a lot harder there. They do math and science and languages in that stream. I think they would prefer the B stream." Mr. Gordon looked in the children's direction, as if implying that the last thing any sane child would want, was to be in the A stream.

"Most children would prefer the line of least resistance if they have a choice," said Curt, supporting Jessica.

"I brought you copies of their last report cards," Jessica said to the vice-principal. He had simply glanced at them, when she gave them to him - obviously not attaching much importance to whatever they contained. Jessica continued, pointing to the documents on the table, "As you can see Mr. Gordon, Jolene has a 90% average." He shrugged his shoulders.

"Sometimes you're comparing apples and oranges," he mumbled.

"Mr. Gordon…I would like both my children to be given a chance in the A stream please." She had learnt from experience you've got to ask for what you want. She put her cards on the table. The vice-principal hesitated.

"They would find it extremely difficult, Mrs. Farrow," he said, folding his arms around his paunchy middle.

"Mrs. Lincoln," Jessica corrected him.

"Oh sorry," he muttered, lowering his eyes and fumbling with the papers on his desk.

"I'm afraid we'll have to consider other possibilities if they can't be given an opportunity in the A stream here," said Jessica, picking up her purse from the floor beside her chair.

Mr. Gordon unfolded his arms and looked from one child to the other.

"Very well" he said, after a short while. "But if they can't keep up, they'll just have to be put in the B stream."

Sadly, Jessica knew that it was not Jolene's high average but Josh's skill on the soccer field, that was the instrument affecting this change of mind.

"Please let us know if they're not keeping up," Jessica added. "Our phone numbers are on the forms you have."

"Yes," said Curt. "If they're not keeping up, we need to be informed. We just don't want them placed in the B stream."

As they left the school that evening, Jessica had a sense of having just participated in an obstacle race. She didn't know it then but getting the children into the A stream was by no means the only hurdle to be overcome at St. Thomas's.

****

There was great excitement in Fleurina's voice as she blurted out over the phone,

"Girl, guess what?"

Before Jessica could respond, Flo continued,

"I'm pregnant, Jess."

Jessica almost fell off her chair. This was fantastic news. She had expected Flo to say she got the position of nurse manager that she had applied for at the hospital where she worked. She never expected this. What was even more coincidental was that Flo's sister, Madge, had confided in Jessica two days ago, that she was pregnant again.

"And not a word to anybody, not even Flo, until after my fifth month," Madge cautioned Jessica. After so many miscarriages, she didn't want to spread the news too soon. True to her word she was taking time off work to give this baby the best chance she could.

"I'm so happy, Jess," Fleurina was saying. "I almost can't believe it."

"Flo…congratulations girl…this is great news…does Madge know yet?"

"Oh please, Jessie…don't say anything to Madge. Chester and I want to hold on to this little secret for as long as we can." *Fat chance.* "But I just had to tell someone…I was bursting with this good news."

"Julian will soon find out…won't he?"

"I hardly see Julian…he drops by once in a blue moon."

"I'm so happy for you and Chester…when are you due?"

"Around Easter," Flo replied and Jessica gulped. That was the same time Madge was also due.

"So how're you feeling?" Jessica wanted to know.

"I'm sick like a dog every morning," she said. "But I'm so happy it doesn't bother me one bit."

"You're going to be one terrific mother, Flo." She longed to tell Flo that Madge was also pregnant and to tell Madge that she had company, but she was not going to break their confidences. They would have to tell each other themselves. She couldn't wait to see their surprised faces.

****

Jessica took Josh and Jo shopping for their fall and winter school clothes. On more than one occasion she had to veto Jolene's choice of clothing which was far too provocative for a thirteen year old. Jolene must have found a way to exchange some of the items. Jessica was going home early one day, towards the second week of school, when she caught sight of her daughter walking home from school in an outfit more suitable for a night club than a school. A pair of tight, black, slinky pants which clung to her like paint was set off by a revealing rose-pink halter top. Tied around her waist was a sweater jacket. Jessica pulled over to the curb and stopped the car.

"Jump in Jo," she shouted. Jolene was obviously surprised and in the car fumbled to get into her jacket. *Okay...I'm not going to freak out.* Jessica had heard that St. Thomas's was considering student uniforms starting next September. Parents as well as students were going to vote on this decision. She regretted it didn't already start this term. This was a move she wholeheartedly approved. She knew exactly how she was going to vote, when the time came. But that was the future. She had an issue to deal with right now.

When they arrived at home, Jolene bounced up the stairs to her bedroom right away. Jessica went to the kitchen. She opened the refrigerator and removed a dish of lasagna she had assembled the night before and placed it into the oven. *Please God.....you put these children in my care. Please grant me the wisdom, the strength and the humility to guide them now.* She began to make a tossed salad, when Jolene entered the kitchen. She had changed her clothes.

"You want any help, Mum?"

"Sure Sweetheart...why don't you mix the juice?" She handed Jolene a can of frozen juice from the freezer. "Where's Josh?" she asked Jolene as she spun the lettuce around in the salad spinner.

"He's probably at soccer practice," Jolene answered. It was not so much what she said or the tone of her voice, but there was something in the way she held her head, that suddenly jolted Jessica to the realization that Jolene was lonely. All her life she had been used to her brother as her constant companion. Now while he was floating on the clouds of soccer stardom, she was alone. Today she was walking home alone from school.

"What's the matter, Darling?" Jessica took a step towards her daughter encircling her in her arms. Jolene put her head on her mother's shoulder and began sobbing loudly.

"I hate it at school, Mum" she said.

"Why Sweetheart?" Jessica asked, gently stroking her daughter's back with one hand. "Are you finding the A steam too hard?"

"The work isn't hard Mum…it's easy."

"Then tell me what's bothering you, Sweetheart."

"They don't like me." A fresh torrent of tears rolled down her cheeks on to Jessica's blouse. "I don't have any friends." It was like a sharp knife piercing her heart. Jessica squeezed Jolene, who was sobbing loudly, to her chest.

After the tears had subsided for a while, Jessica asked Jolene to take her through a typical day at school.

"Tell me what goes on, Darling…from the time you reach to school in the morning."

"I stay by myself, Mum. No one wants to talk to me."

"Not even Josh?"

"All those girls are all over Josh, Mum. He doesn't have time for me." Jessica could tell that Jolene was fighting back a fresh torrent of tears.

"Do you try to talk to anyone, yourself?"

"They have their own cliques Mum…they don't want me in them."

"How do you know that?"

"Mum today at lunch time, in the cafeteria…I went to sit at the end of a long table and one girl there told me that seat was already taken."

"Well maybe it was." Jessica was trying to see life from the other point of view also.

"I went to another table and sat all by myself. Even when I left the cafeteria, nobody took the seat that was 'taken'. They just didn't want me there."

Jessica could see clearly now that Jolene was lonely and trying desperately to fit in. Perhaps those 'night club' clothes were simply a means of drawing attention to herself, so she could become one of the crowd. Her heart felt like lead.

"You are a bright, smart, beautiful girl, Jo. Don't let anybody make you believe otherwise." She heard the voice of her father talking to her many years ago. How soothing and inspiring it felt at the time. She hoped these words were having a similar effect on Jolene today. She took her hands in both of hers and continued, "You don't need to dress in a provocative way to show it, Jo. It's in you - it's part and parcel of you." Jolene was listening attentively. She knew her mother had seen the sexy outfit she wore to school that day. Far from winning her friends, it only spurred the wrath of her home room teacher, who ordered her to cover up herself. "Be proud of who you are Jo and be kind to others."

"All I need is one good friend, Mum" Jolene whimpered.

"I'm sure if you look around not everybody is in a clique. Why don't you befriend one of these."

"I tried Mum. I met this girl called Hega." She stopped as Jessica waited to hear what became of her friendship with Hega.

"As if I want to hear all about Hega Smith's sex life" she said, throwing up her eyes in disgust.

"You chose the wrong person," went on Jessica. "But I'm sure if you keep an open mind, you may find someone you can be friends with."

"Mmhmm." Jolene did not contradict her.

"Perhaps those 'clique' girls are just like Hega," Jessica continued. Jolene actually smiled.

"And Sweetheart, make sure to be the first to sit at an empty table in the cafeteria…and don't move for anyone." While she wanted her daughter to be kind, she didn't want her to be a 'push over'. She had to equip her with the tools of the trade to take care of herself. "If anyone tells you that seat is taken, tell them of course it's taken - by you."

While Jolene was in the shower that night, Jessica found a few moments to have a private conversation with Josh.

"You guys are in new surroundings," she told him. "So watch out for Jo at break time and lunch time…and just make sure she's okay. Right?" She didn't want to detract from his current 'star' status, which may or may not be beneficial to him, but she was determined to keep a close eye on both her children. She and Curt were planning to attend the first parent-teacher's meeting next week.

"Sure Mum," replied Josh. He never saw Jo at these times but he was going to look out for her.

Almost immediately Jessica noticed a change in Jolene. She found friends that she liked. The clothes she chose to wear to school were now far more suitable. Perhaps it was because of the cold weather but that rose pink halter top never made an appearance again. Jolene became a lot more contented with the school.

****

The government in Grenada was finally overthrown by Maurice Bishop and the New Jewel Movement. Grenadians had suffered immensely from twelve years of a dictatorship which left the people scarred, the treasury empty, and the infrastructure and economy of the island in shambles.

Many times Grandma wondered what was the point of installing electricity and running water at home, when almost on a weekly basis electricity would be cut off. If you wanted water from the taps, you had to turn them on well after midnight. Sure now she had a flush toilet and a beautiful shower stall, but what was the point when there was no water? She felt tired and frustrated. But maybe things would get a little better now. All those big, gaping pot holes in the main road will be repaired. It would take time. All she had to do was wait and see.

But she had a lot to be thankful for still. Jessica and the twins were doing well. She hoped she could see Jessica just one more time before God claimed her. She wanted to tell her how special she was. She had so much to thank Jessica for. And she wanted to tell her everything about her mother's illness - but just in case - one never knew, she was going to put it in writing and leave everything in her trunk, together with her will, for Jessica.

When Julian heard the news of the coup, he toyed with the idea of returning to his homeland. Although there were many aspects of Canada that he liked - there was a dark side to it, that really bothered him. Twice in the past six months he was stopped by the police late at night for no apparent reason. On the first occasion he was really scared when two policemen approached him and ordered him out of his car. He remembered Chester's warning to be very careful where he placed his hands "as after they shoot you, they are likely to say that they thought you were reaching for a weapon." The second time Julian was stopped, he had a white girl with him and something - he suspected it was her presence - seemed to enrage the police officer. Both were ordered out of the car and down on the ground for what seemed like an eternity.

"I can't take this bullshit anymore," Julian said to Flo afterwards.

Now that the NJM had seized power - a move Julian was convinced the majority of Grenadians supported - he wondered whether he wouldn't be better off in his native land.

"There are problems of one sort or the other, everywhere in this world," Chester warned him. "You can't keep running. Sometimes you just have to take a stand and fight for what you believe in."

****

Madge was the first of the sisters to give birth to a six pound baby girl by cesarean section. It had been a difficult pregnancy but Willie, as well as Jessica, Curt, Jolene and Josh, were always there for her. Throughout her long labour both Willie and Jessica stayed with her. Finally after a number of hours, the decision was made to take her to surgery and a short while later a healthy, beautiful baby girl was born.

Flo had been calling all along and was being kept informed of Madge's progress. Jessica could never determine which one of the sisters was more shocked by the news of the other's pregnancy, four months ago.

"You mean, you knew Flo was pregnant all this time and you never said one word to me?" Madge asked surprised, but she had to admit that Jessica kept her confidence as faithfully as she'd kept Flo's.

Ten days later, Chester called to say that Flo was in labour. That night she gave birth to an eight pound baby boy. They named him Chester Cyprian. The two sisters were overjoyed as were their relatives in Grenada, where great rejoicing and celebrating were taking place. They couldn't wait to get together to show off their beautiful bundles of joy.

"Let's surprise Ma Hilly, Mammie and Daddy...and let's all go home on a holiday together," suggested Flo.

Jessica had already decided that she was overdue for a visit to Grenada as was Madge who, now that she had a baby to show off, was just as keen. Flo's idea of going home together and surprising the folks was slowly gathering momentum.

****

That summer Curt decided it was time to finish the basement. The previous year Josh and Jolene watched, and sometimes helped Willie to do his basement. They were thrilled by Curt's decision. Now it was their turn.

"I'm good at painting, Uncle Curt" said Jolene.

"I helped Uncle Willie wire his whole basement," announced Josh proudly. Jessica didn't want the process to take a lifetime and was more inclined to get the entire project done professionally and speedily, but seeing how keen everyone was, agreed to compromise. Not only would it save money but she saw another big positive - this project was bringing Curt much closer to the children, especially Jolene. In recent months, if he wasn't complaining about all the junk food they were stuffing themselves with, it was their habits of leaving their rooms and bathroom in 'a downright mess'. Sometimes when he spoke to them, there was an edge to his voice, which he couldn't contain.

"You have to learn how to speak to the children," Jessica chided him, and deep down Curt had to admit she had a point.

They drew up several plans for the basement and finally settled on a simple one that everyone in the family loved. The children wanted a big room that could house a pool table or ping-pong table. Jessica wanted to make sure that there was sufficient storage room and another bedroom and bathroom that could be used for guests. Even though Grandma couldn't come to visit, Debbie had promised to come sometime, as well as Trevor, her dear little brother, who now attended the University of the West Indies; and several of Curt's cousins from Nova Scotia. She wanted to be prepared for them. Curt wanted a quiet area where he could listen to his music and it was important to him and everyone that the finished product was well lit and inviting.

A professional was hired to break the concrete and do the drywall. Willie dropped by in his overalls many weekends to help and Curt saw the remarkable - both

Josh and Jo were exceptional. Jolene was an excellent painter and decorator. She had a keen eye. Josh was an all-rounder. He did most of the electrical wiring as well as the wood work. They both took pride in their work and at its completion, everyone was delighted with the finished product.

****

On a busy Monday morning at work, just before she rushed off to a staff meeting, Jessica received a phone call from St. Thomas's high school. *Oh my God…something must have happened to one of the children.* She took the receiver nervously.

"Hello."

"Mrs. Lincoln…this is Mr. Roman, Josh's soccer coach."

"Yes…Is anything wrong with him?" she asked, almost in a whisper. Her heart was beating quickly and a vision of Josh lying hurt somewhere flashed across her eyes.

"Oh he's fine, Mrs. Lincoln" said Mr. Roman and Jessica exhaled. "I'm calling because Josh informed me you won't allow him to play in the end of term games this semester."

Jessica sat down. She gestured to her staff member to go ahead to the meeting without her. "I'll soon be there" she mimed.

"Did he tell you why I said that Mr. Roman?" Jessica couldn't believe her ears. It was the first time a teacher was calling her about one of the children. When Josh brought home his mid term results with 43% in math and 56% in English, Jessica was upset. Some action had to be taken immediately. She knew he was capable of much better. She was convinced when he said to her outright " Mum…studying is for nerds. It's not the cool thing to do."

"Okay," Jessica told Josh. "If those marks don't improve right away, trust me…you won't be playing soccer in the end of term tournament."
Mr. Roman cleared his throat, then replied,
"Mrs. Lincoln, he'll be letting down his teammates and his school very badly if he doesn't play in these end of term matches."

"I understand that, Mr. Roman." She stopped to take a deep breath. She wanted to scream. "But I'm sure you also understand he'll be letting down himself and his family even worse, if he doesn't do much better in math and English?"

"He's our star player Mrs. Lincoln."
Jessica knew this was an attempt at flattery to appease her. "Mr. Roman…I'm willing to play ball with you." Jessica felt she had clout on her side. "If we can encourage Josh so that he takes his academic subjects seriously and improves his marks significantly, I'll be willing to allow him to play soccer for the team."
Mr. Roman hesitated. "I'll do what I can but you should be talking to his other teachers," he said.

"That's true. I'll be seeing them at the parent-teacher's meeting on Wednesday. But make no mistake…for me, that's where the priority lies."

By the end of the conversation, Jessica was convinced that if Josh's math and English teachers showed half as much interest as his soccer coach showed in her son's performance on the soccer field, he would be doing much better in those subjects. Happily right now, Jo seemed to be doing fairly well. She enjoyed spending time at Madge's, now that the new baby was here. It was like a see-saw. When one child was up, the other was down and vice versa.

Jessica had to admit that talking to Josh's teachers about their expectations for him was positive. At the parent-teacher's meeting, she and Curt devised means and measures with the teachers that could help Josh. She finally got the sense that they were a team working together for her son's benefit.

The job was far from easy. Josh hated his literature book, which Jessica took the time to read. At the conclusion of the book she understood why some children feel marginalized in the school system. They are not included. They do not see themselves reflected anywhere. Certainly not in the prescribed literature books.

"I know why Josh can't stand that book," Jessica said to Curt as they lay in bed that night.

"Why? What's wrong with it?"

"Nothing...but the subject matter is soo..." she groped for the proper word. "Distant."

"In what way?"

"Well... it's about this cranky ol' lady... passing gas."

Curt smiled.

"Too bad" he said, "there isn't a choice of books for the students."

"That would be so nice...but with all the cutbacks in education..."

"Yes...that almighty budget. I hear they're thinking of phasing out gym and music teachers now."

"That will be terrible...it will just open up another can of worms."

"At the next parent-teacher's meeting, we should find out how the literature books are chosen. There are a few I would like to suggest."

"At least there is some literary advantage to the current one...and I tried to point that out to Josh."

Curt put his arms around Jessica and pulled her to him.

"Josh will be okay," he said. "We just have to hang in there with him...and Sweetheart, you're doing one terrific job."

Jessica buried her head into Curt's chest. Those few words of encouragement were so comforting. They gave her the strength and the determination she needed to continue.

CHAPTER 24

It was almost impossible for everyone to get time off from work at the same time for the trip home to Grenada. Jessica wanted to go in the summer or at Christmas, when Curt and the twins could accompany her. That was the worst time for Flo and Chester. After taking almost two years off, Madge was reluctant to request prime vacation time in the summer, from her job. So plans had to be redone. Flo, Chester and Little Chet along with Madge and her daughter, Ayanna, were going home at the end of February - in the peak of winter. Getting away during those severe winter months was very appealing to Madge. Even though he couldn't go too, Willie encouraged Madge to go along with her sister.

Jessica and her family decided to go home in the summer. The twins were now sixteen years old and Grandma and Aunt Mattie would be overjoyed to see them all.

"Too bad we couldn't all go together," Madge said, upon her return from Grenada.

"We will…sometime…but this time, I just want to hold Grandma and give her a great big hug and kiss and thank you," said Jessica.

"You should see Ayanna and LilChet with Mammie " said Madge. Little Chet's name had gone from Little Chester to Little Chet and had gradually settled on LilChet.

"Yes?"

"She spoil dem for so!"

"I'm sure they just loved it," Jessica laughed.

"You could say dat again."

Although there were signs of neglect in many parts of the island, their visit to Grenada was a happy one. Just being with family and friends was all that was needed. The annual Bailey beach picnic, which had lapsed for a number of years, took place during their visit.

"And you wouldn't believe who's Mammie's good friend now," continued Madge.

"Who?"

"Aunt Mattie oui!" Three weeks in Grenada and Madge had relapsed hook, line and sinker into the Grenadian twang.

"Yes?"

"She look so different now…you should see yoh Aunt Mattie."

"Madge girl, do you know it's been twelve years already since I left home?" Jessica could hardly wait for July third when with Curt and the twins, she too would be heading towards Grenada.

****

The doorbell rang at about nine p.m. on the last day of April. Jessica peeped through the drapes and saw Madge's car in the driveway. What's Madge doing here at this time on a cold and dreary night when she has to get up early in the morning for work? Jessica wondered, as she went towards the door. Curt was two steps behind her. One look at Madge's face told Jessica that something was dreadfully wrong.

"What's the matter?" she asked nervously.

"Let's go in and sit down" said Madge, taking off her coat with help from Curt.

"Hi Auntie Madge," said Jolene coming down the stairs. She stopped short when she noticed her aunt's face.

Jessica led the way to the living room. They sat down.

"Ayanna and Willie okay?" she asked.

"They're fine."

"You're okay?"

"I'm fine," said Madge. This was going to be hard. This was one bit of news she did not relish being the bearer of. She didn't know where to start. She looked at Jessica and blurted out,

"I just got a phone call from Mammie…" she said. "Ma Hilly just passed away."

Jessica heard what Madge said but it was as if this was a dream and she didn't really hear.

"Who passed away?" she asked as if from a distance. She heard Jolene screaming and crying far away, "Grandma?…no…NO…NO!"

She thought she saw her mother Audrey lying on a bed looking painfully thin. Or was that herself? Somebody was holding her up…fanning her face…putting water to her lips.

Jessica came to and realized that Curt and Madge were leaning over her and Curt was holding a cup of water to her lips. She must have blacked out for a few minutes.

"What happened?" she asked looking around at Josh and Jolene who were both weeping, while looking at her concerned. Nobody answered, but she had to know.

"What did you say Madge?" she asked again. Madge looked at Curt, unsure whether she should repeat what she had said. Jessica kept looking into her eyes.

"Did you say that Grandma passed away?" Madge nodded and Curt held Jessica by the shoulders. Jo and Josh came towards her and together they cried and dabbed at each others tears and cried some more.

"We were going to see her in two months...only two months," Jessica said half to herself. In fact, the following day Curt was going to get their plane tickets.

Mrs. Bailey and some other neighbours were with Aunt Mattie and Shark, when Jessica phoned home. Grandma did not suffer, they assured her. She got up as usual that morning. In the evening after she'd eaten she went to sit on the verandah. Aunt Mattie was with her when she suddenly slumped over in the chair. By the time Aunt Mattie shouted for help which came almost immediately, Grandma had passed away.

"All she been talkin' 'bout dese days is y'all comin' home to visit," said Aunt Mattie. Jessica had originally intended to surprise her grandmother, but once the Bailey sisters went home, she could contain this news no longer. She told her grandmother the exact date and time they were coming. As Jessica was speaking on the phone to Aunt Mattie, her father arrived. He spoke to Jessica and offered to get the funeral arrangements on the way.

"Thanks so much, Dad...I'll call you tomorrow as soon as I have a flight," she told him.

Jessica, Joshua and Jolene left from Toronto via a direct flight to Grenada that Friday morning. The funeral was scheduled for Saturday afternoon. Jessica was able to arrange for some of her vacation time to be brought forward by two months. Since the children were in the middle of their school semester, they were booked to return the following Wednesday. They would have missed less than five days of school. Not being able to cancel important events, Curt stayed behind.

"It will be good to have you there for the children when they return," Jessica agreed with him.

After the initial shock and flood of tears, Jessica was doing much better. She contacted her travel agency and booked the earliest flight available to Grenada. She packed her own luggage and supervised the packing of the children's. She spoke to their teachers at school and arranged that whatever lessons or assignments they missed would be made up the following week. She phoned and discussed several details with Aunt Mattie, her father and the manager of the funeral parlor.

They arrived in Grenada at three p.m. Ian was at the airport to meet them. His hair was all gray now as was his mustache. Jessica hugged her father warmly.

"It's so good to see you, Daddy" she said. "It's been too long."

"Hi Pa," Josh and Jo said to him as they embraced. There was a noticeable warmth between her father and the twins.

"You look great, Jessie" he said, surprised by this gorgeous woman with flawless nutmeg-coloured skin. Her majestic bearing reminded him of her grandmother. Turning to Josh and Jo he said "I don't believe it's just three short years since I've seen these children. They've grown so much."

He drove them up to Rockville where Mr. and Mrs. Bailey, their daughter Terri, Jacob and Aunt Mattie and several other neighbours were waiting to welcome them. Aunt Mattie had changed a lot - she seemed much more 'tuned in' than before. Gone was that spaced out, brown-dressed woman she used to know. There was not much change in Ma Bailey and Mr. Bailey. Jacob gave them all a welcoming smile. He too was now gray-haired.

The streets to Rockville seemed narrower and more curvy. The hill up to Grandma's home seemed steeper than Jessica remembered it. The huge flat area where she used to play cricket and rounders with the Bailey children, now seemed rugged and tiny. But she gasped at the magnificent view from the top of the hill. She never before appreciated just how picture card beautiful it was. On one side reigned the Mount Gozo mountains in all their splendor while on the other was a spectacular view down hill and up vale all the way to Point Saline. Red blossoms of numerous flamboyant trees, competing with the brilliance of bougainvillea blossoms, nestled amidst these valleys and hills. *This place is absolutely dazzling!*

The house was as neat as ever. Her photograph, as well as those of the children, were prominently displayed on a wall unit in the living room. She saw the big *Frigidaire* refrigerator in the dining room. She saw the new bathroom that Mr. Bailey built for Grandma. There were several buckets of water in the shower stall. *For when there's no water in the taps.* The 'big' bedroom which brought back a host of memories to her, still had the children's bunk beds as well as Grandma's mahogany bed and 'trunk' dresser at the opposite side of the room. They were all neatly made up. She saw the bedspreads, curtains, towels, dishes, pots and pans that she had sent over the years. But there was no Grandma. A wave of emptiness threatened to envelop Jessica. She was home now…but there was no Grandma.

She heard the children talking to someone on the verandah, and recognized Shark's voice. The kitchen door opened and she heard him enter. She went out to greet him.

"Hi Shark," she said and lightly embraced him. He was now balding with a scruffy, scraggly beard. Jessica recognized the shirt he was wearing. It was one that Curt had found much too 'loud' for him, so she included it in the barrel she sent home last Christmas. Although Shark himself never wrote to her, every now and again he would get his mother to do his dirty work. Aunt Mattie wrote a few times begging for one thing or the other for Shark. Once it was for a tape recorder; another time for a pair of binoculars or a hunting knife. It wasn't enough that for practically all his life the women in the house put bread into his big mouth; he demanded cake with icing on it too!

"Hi Jessica," he replied. What seemed to be a smile rested for a brief unaccustomed moment on his face before it quickly disappeared.

"So how are you, Shark?"

"I's fine," he answered.

"Were you there when Grandma passed away?" She knew the answer but thought she'd ask anyway. She wanted to ask him about his longtime woman - Miss Lucy - but thought better of it.

"No...but I come soon after." Shark hesitated briefly. "She was aw'right the las' time I seen her... laughin' an' talkin' an' everyt'in'."
Jessica nodded.

"Mum," said Josh, coming inside. "Jacob just showed me where they buried Spice." Spice died two weeks ago. Grandma was as attached to her as were the twins.

Supper was down at the Baileys that evening. Jessica decided to turn in to bed early as fatigue was beginning to take hold of her. She was pleased to see the new friendship that had developed between Aunt Mattie and Ma Bailey - especially now that Grandma had passed away. Josh and Jo slept on their old beds, while Jessica curled up on Grandma's mahogany bed. But she couldn't sleep. Strange but she never before noticed the noisiness of a tropical night. There seemed to be a whole orchestra out there with frogs, birds, crickets and other insects all competing - each one determined to outdo the other in intensity.

****

Around midday Jessica and the twins went to the funeral parlor in St. George's to see Grandma. They wanted to spend time alone with Grandma before the official viewing at one thirty. They took Lenox Bailey's new minibus. He no longer had the bus *Sensational*. Although Lenox still lived at home with his parents, it was a well known fact that he had two women and two different families, between which he did a balancing act. Fascinatingly enough, both these women were close friends. Their friendship began many years ago, when

Lenox attempted to marry a young girl from 'overseas' called Daisy. These two women joined forces solidly against Daisy, who had no choice but to give up Lenox and return to her homeland.

They walked from the Market Square to the funeral parlor on Sea street. Sweat ran down Jessica's back as the sun beat mercilessly down on them. She was thankful she didn't bother to wear any pantyhose. The town was busy and congested. Lots of young people were just hanging around. There was far too much traffic for the narrow little streets. But there was something warm and intimate just being there. She enjoyed that fresh, salty smell from the sea nearby which mingled with the spicy aromas from the products of the vendors in the outdoor market and sweetly permeated the atmosphere.

"Darlin'…leh me fix dat for you," a total stranger said to Jessica as she fixed the zipper, at the back of her skirt, that was coming down a tiny bit.

"Thank you," Jessica replied surprised. She had forgotten how friendly and personal Grenadians were. Twelve years ago this would not have surprised her in the least.

As they turned the corner onto Sea street, a dirty, red-eyed bum came towards them. Jessica was about to cross to the other side of the street when something made her take a second look. She gasped. It was Jack DeCoutreau. She was embarrassed that the children had seen him too. Did they know who this was? She got her answer from Jolene's tightening grip around her mother's arm and Josh looking stiffly in the opposite direction. She had a lot of explaining to do. But not now.

Jack must have recognized Jessica because he followed them across to the other side of the street. He seemed to be begging. More to get rid of him rather than any sense of wanting to deal with him, Jessica fumbled in her purse and pulled out a note. It was a ten dollar note but she gave it to him anyway to get rid of him quickly.

"Thanks," he mumbled. There was no hint whatsoever of the old Jack she once loved. She knew little of his life in England but he was a broken man now. The once talented, debonair Jack that everyone worshipped was a sad alcoholic today.

"He's always begging people, Mum" Josh said with irritation.

"Do you know who that is?"

"Sure. Before we went to Canada," Jolene said, "We met him in town one day. He said he was our father and asked if he could borrow a dollar."

Jessica stopped short in her tracks. *I don't believe this.*

"You actually met him?" she asked. "Grandma never told me this."

"We never told Grandma," Josh replied. "She never knew."

No wonder the children had a hard time accepting a daddy figure in their lives. At first they seemed so resistant to accepting Curt as their new father. She distinctly remembered Jo saying to her "I don't need no Daddy." It was all falling into place.

"We have a lot to talk about" she said to them. *It's high time.*

****

Grandma looked as though she were asleep, and having beautiful dreams. There was the hint of a smile on her face. She wore a pale blue dress that Jessica had sent to her. Two tiny pearls decorated her earlobes with a matching strand around her neck. Her makeup was artfully done. There was no need for Jessica to fix anything.

They all three knelt together at the kneeler beside the coffin.

"I wanted to tell you thanks, Grandma. I wanted to hug you and kiss you and tell you thanks. But I was too late...too late..." Jessica's tears were flowing freely now. "Thanks for love, Ma...thanks for being there for all of us. You took care of Mummy during her illness. You were there for me and for Josh and Jo...I could not have done it without you, Ma. You propped me up when I was down. You taught me so much." Jessica was aware of Josh and Jo hugging her and they too were crying.

"We'll always remember you, Grandma" said Jo. "How you read us stories and poems and letters from Mummy...how you encouraged us at school...took care of us."

"You were the best grandmother anyone could ever have...we're going to miss you soo much." Josh was sobbing on Jessica's shoulder.

They spent the full hour privately expressing what needed to be expressed - telling Grandma how much she meant to them and how very much she was going to be missed. At one o' clock Aunt Mattie and Shark arrived. Jessica had arranged for Shark to drive the limousine the family would use - a job he was most delighted to have.

"So long as you're not drinking any alcohol, Shark" she warned him.

"Not a drop," he agreed, making a face as if Jessica had suggested the most ridiculous and far fetched idea in the world.

"I'm gwine miss Hilda bad Jessie…mih only sister gone." Aunt Mattie looked so bewildered. Hilda and Matilda. Two sisters that were there for each other through thick and thin. Now the older sister was gone. Jessica knew how lonesome the remaining one must be feeling. She put her arms around Aunt Mattie.

By one thirty five other members of the public who knew Grandma or Jessica or any family member began to show up gradually. They shook hands and accepted hugs and kisses and condolences from scores of people. Ian came with Albertine. Had she not been with her father, Jessica might not have recognized Albertine. She had lost a lot of weight and was certainly no longer the glamour queen of yesteryear.

"Accept mih sympathy, Jessie."

"Thanks Albertine," Jessica replied, bending slightly to accept a peck on the cheek and lightly hugging her stepmother. "It's good to see you…how are you?" Albertine looked surprised by this warm and unexpected response from Jessica. She recalled those days when Jessica lived at Willow Lane and felt ashamed of herself. What an idiot she had been back then.

"I doin' fine, Jessie" she answered with a shy smile. "Trevor and Debbie say to tell you and the children how'dy."

A short, light-skinned, shabbily dressed woman approached Jessica.

"Accept my sympathy," she said to everyone in the receiving line. When she got to Jessica, she paused a while longer. *Should I know this person?*

"Thank you," Jessica said to her, shaking her hand.

"I see you don't recognize me," she said, looking up at Jessica and not letting go of her hand. Then added before Jessica could apologize for her bad memory. "Louisa." Jessica was shocked. This was Jack's wife - Louisa DeCoutreau. They stood looking at each other for a while.

"Louisa!...My God, it's been ages. Thanks for coming, Louisa...it's so good to see you."

"I had to come," she said. She was still holding Jessica's hand. "I wanted to tell you, Jessica, that you were the fortunate one - when you think life is being unkind to you, sometimes it's being good to you. You just can't see it at the time."

She left to mingle with the crowd and to partake of the soft drinks and finger foods in another area - a puny, little woman who years ago thought she'd got the prize. Indeed, back then, Jessica also believed that by getting Jack, Louisa won the prize. She came today to tell Jessica that that wasn't so. Jessica's misfortune then was life's way of giving her a gift. She couldn't see it then but it was crystal clear now.

Grandma was taken up to Rockville and after a beautiful service at *Our lady of Fatima's* church was taken to the Rockville cemetery. Almost everyone in the community came out to pay their last respects. Grandma lived most of her eighty three years in Rockville. She was known to just about everyone. Jessica greeted many people she recognized from her childhood. The grave diggers, eyes glazed from drinking too much strong rum, were the same ones she knew as a child. In fact when the coffin couldn't fit in the prepared hole, because of a big stone in the ground, everything seemed like *deja vu*. She had seen this happen many times in the past. This was one point she had forgotten to ask her father to check out.

"It won't take much adjusting," Ian said to Jessica, after consulting with the grave diggers who were now busily digging in the opposite end from the stone. The priest said the final prayers, gave his blessing and left. The church choir joined by many others, continued singing hymns.

Finally the hole was ready and the coffin was lowered into it. It was the last and final goodbye. This moment would have been very sad were it not for the drama of a fat lady attempting to get into the hole with her long time friend, Hilda.

"Oh mih Gawd…Hilda I comin' wid you too," she cried. "I comin' now, now Hilda…Wah!…wahwahwah!" The woman slipped deeper and deeper into the hole. People at the back of the gathering pushed closer to get a better view. The woman got down into the grave and lay wailing on the coffin. Eventually when she thought she had created a big enough spectacle, she dried her tears and tried to get out of the hole. But it was too deep and too slippery - she couldn't get back out easily. When no one was offering her a helping hand, she began loud cussing, much to the amusement of the onlookers. Jolene had her hand to her mouth trying to keep back the giggles.

"But Miss Muzzie" one onlooker said, earning for himself a severe 'bad eye' from the woman. "We t'ought you want to go wid Miss Hilly."

make me so happy. Always. I dont want to go without letting you know how I feel. Jessica was dabbing at her eyes now. *I know your children is in the best hands possible. That is the kind of woman you are.* Jessica stopped to blow her nose and dry her eyes some more. *I never before tell you, so nobody will shun you, that youre poor mother died of consumption.* Jessica was three years old when her mother passed away and she was finally discovering the cause of her death. When she was a little girl, to have tuberculosis or consumption, was to be labeled an untouchable. Grandma had purposely kept this information from Jessica and everyone else. She had quietly taken Audrey away from the island during the latter stage of her illness, leaving Jessica in the care of Aunt Mattie during that period. *All you can do in life, is the best you know how. You cant help the sadness that is part of life. Just make sure you get some joy in between. You can still enjoy the beautiful roses even though the rose bush full up of nasty thorns. I get a good life Jessie and I wish the same for you and yourse.*

    It was as though Grandma was talking to her from beyond. It was a sad yet happy feeling. Grandma had said she'd had a good life. Jessica was most grateful for that. She felt lucky to have known this woman. She may have been a woman of modest means but she was a strong and capable woman with a heart like no other. Hilda Thorne, her grandmother, was an exceptional woman.

    The last task Jessica handled before her return trip, was her grandmother's will. The property was left to Jessica. She assured Aunt Mattie that it was her wish as well as Grandma's that she remain in the home. Neither was she to worry about finances. Jessica would continue to support her aunt from abroad, since she had no other reliable means of support. Shark, it seems, was a turncoat. After the fall of the Gairy government, he had joined the new party in power. He was being trained as a soldier in the army, Jessica was told.

****

Back in Ottawa the weather was beginning to show signs of spring. After a bitterly cold winter, everyone was relieved. This exposure to extremes conditioned the people of Ottawa to appreciate and enjoy warmer weather, whenever it made an appearance. Bicyclists, joggers and walkers with their pets competed for space in the parks. Occasionally the wind brought the whiff of some delicious barbecue in the neighbourhood to their nostrils.

Curt met Jessica at the airport, on her return from Grenada. Once again she felt a sense of gratitude. This fine, loving and honourable man was her husband. She remembered the Jack DeCoutreau she had fallen in love with decades ago and the bum she recently encountered in Grenada. Life certainly takes many turns and twists.

"It's so good to have you back," said Curt.

"It's good to be with you...my Darling," Jessica said as she hugged and kissed him.

"How are the children?" she asked.

"They're okay...they had only a few assignments to make up when they got back."

By the time they arrived home from the airport, the children had already come home from school. They were both getting supper ready. They left what they were doing to rush to the door to greet their mother. At supper that night, Curt heard all about Grandma's farewell and the trip to Grenada in general. The children had given him news of Aunt Mattie, Shark and the Baileys down the hill.

"Is it true a woman tried to get buried with Grandma?" he asked. Josh and Jo had filled him in on this story, with lots of embellishments.

"I don't think she actually wanted to get buried. She just wanted to be dramatic," Jessica answered.

"Uncle Curt it went from 'I comin' wid you Hilda, now...now!' to 'get me out a dis f---ing hole now...okay boy?'" Josh tried to imitate Miss Muzzie's antics. He was quite the comedian. They were all squealing with laughter.

They spoke of the surprise meeting with Trevor and later Debbie at Grand Anse beach. Pa had arranged this surprise, Jolene said. They all had an energizing early morning dip. Even Albertine came to offer her sympathy. She was not like before; she had changed both in appearance and demeanor.

Later that week, Jessica spoke to her children about Jack. She described how she'd met him and what he was like at that time. She mentioned what a great soccer player he'd been, not unlike Josh today.

"It was a brief period in my life," she said. "It should not have happened ...but it did...and I do not regret it...because here I am today...with two beautiful, fantastic children."

They listened attentively but said nothing. They seemed curious yet a bit uncomfortable.

"Ask me whatever you wish about your father," Jessica finally said. "And I will try to answer."

"Our biological father," Jolene corrected her.

"That's right," Jessica agreed. "Jack has never been your father...the most we can say is that he is your biological father."

"Mum" said Josh, clearing his throat. "Do you think I will end up like Jack because he's my biological father?"

"What?"

"Well...I have his genes..." There was a slight quiver near his mouth as he spoke. Jessica regretted the soccer comparison, she'd made a moment ago.

"Certainly not," she answered right away. "Life is mostly about choices. Our genes may predispose us towards a certain direction, but nine times out of ten we can choose whether or not we go there.

"God may give someone the gift of intelligence... that person may choose to develop it or not...that person may choose alcohol instead...now does that mean that person has no control over what he or she becomes?" She stopped for a moment to see if both children were with her on this.

"That's right," said Jolene. "You can't help it if you have the gene for diabetes, but you can certainly help what you put in your mouth."

Josh nodded.

"And to talk about Jack specifically...I believe he made the choice to start drinking...and it gradually became an addiction."

Both Josh and Jo nodded.

"In Grenada he was a great soccer player, and everyone was constantly singing his praises and bowing down before him. Why study? he thought. What's the point? So he flunked out of high school. But when his soccer days were over, Jack had nothing...not one thing...to fall back on."

Suddenly, it clicked with Joshua why his mother and great-grandmother always insisted that he study and do well academically. God gave you the brains, they said to him over and over and over. Use them.

****

October 1983 was the darkest period in the history of Grenada. The New Jewel Movement had condemned the old regime but many people felt they didn't do much better when in office. There was a split in the party when Maurice Bishop, the prime minister, rejected a proposal for joint leadership with the second-in-command. This resulted in Bishop being placed under house arrest by this rival camp, of which Shark was an ardent supporter.

The people revolted. They freed Bishop from his captors and took him up to Fort Rupert. Three armoured vehicles - it was suspected that Shark was in one of these - arrived at Fort Rupert, firing into the crowd. Many people, including Maurice Bishop, lost their lives that day. It was as though a monster breathing fire was roaming rampant in the streets.

Like all Grenadians abroad, Jessica heard this news with great shock and disbelief. The people were traumatized like never before. Her father and stepmother were trapped in their homes, as the entire island was under a curfew. While in the country areas like Rockville, one could get around this ruling, the people in St. George's had no option. Ma Bailey told of several youngsters who could not be accounted for by grieving relatives. She thanked God that Julian was away because knowing her youngest son, he would have been in the thick of this.

Jessica spoke to Aunt Mattie. She hadn't seen Shark in ages but heard the rumour that he had been incarcerated along with many others. Surprisingly she seemed resigned to whatever his fate was.

"He's mih son and I gwine always love him…but sometimes you have to pay for yoh bad doin's," she said sadly to Jessica.

****

It was graduation day at St. Thomas's high school. It was the day Jessica had been dreaming of for years. Sometimes she wondered whether it would ever come to pass. It was finally here. After breakfast that morning, before they went to the school for the graduation ceremony, Josh and Jo were each presented with a small box - a little gift from their parents. Each of them unwrapped their gift and opened a velvet box. In each box lay a beautiful golden bracelet at the center of which was a heart encircling the letter J.

"It's gorgeous," said Jolene.

"Wow! This is spiffy! Where did y'all get these?" asked Josh. Josh's bracelet was the masculine version of Jolene's.

"Let's just say it's the symbol of our undying love for you both," answered Jessica as Curt stood beside her smiling.

The school principal read the names of the students as each one stepped up to the podium to receive his or her high school diploma. The school auditorium was crowded.

"Jolene Farrow."

"Joshua Farrow."

Sitting in the audience, with Jessica and Curt were Madge, Willie, Flo, Chester and Trevor, who was now doing post graduate studies at York University in Toronto. Jessica grasped Curt's hand tightly. They had done it. The first part of the journey was completed. Both youngsters had been accepted at renowned universities in Canada, to continue their studies. Joshua was interested in computer engineering, while Jolene had chosen architecture.

Later that evening at home, there was a dinner to celebrate the children's success.

"We have to celebrate each step on the ladder of success," Jessica said to Flo, when she'd called to invite them to the children's graduation. Julian arrived for the dinner with Ayanna and LilChet. He had been baby-sitting them at Madge's home during the long graduation ceremony. They were two gorgeous children who reminded Jessica of her twins many years ago.

Jessica looked around at the gathering. She was so thankful. Here were her darling children, her loving husband who had stood by and encouraged her; Trevor, whom she still called her 'little' brother and those caring friends who were always there with some kind word of support and encouragement. They were a source of inspiration - a mentor to her and the children. She could not have done it without them. Jessica felt that her grandmother and mother were smiling down on them.

"Let's give thanks to God for this day" she said, as with bowed heads, they all held hands.

ISBN 141201529-4